J

The Squibob Papers

SALZWASSER
VERLAG

John Phoenix

The Squibob Papers

Reprint of the original, first published in 1865.

1st Edition 2022 | ISBN: 978-3-75259-052-4

Verlag (Publisher): Salzwasser Verlag GmbH, Zeilweg 44, 60439 Frankfurt, Deutschland
Vertretungsberechtigt (Authorized to represent): E. Roepke, Zeilweg 44, 60439 Frankfurt, Deutschland
Druck (Print): Books on Demand GmbH, In de Tarpen 42, 22848 Norderstedt, Deutschland

THE

SQUIBOB PAPERS.

BY

JOHN PHŒNIX.

AUTHOR OF "PHŒNIXIANA."

WITH COMIC ILLUSTRATIONS BY THE AUTHOR.

NEW YORK

MDCCCLXV.

TO

GEN. GEO. B. McCLELLAN,

THE FRIEND AND CLASSMATE OF THE AUTHOR,

THESE SKETCHES

ARE AFFECTIONATELY DEDICATED.

A Side Elevation of G. Washington.—*See page* 36.
(*not* by Gilbert Stuart.)

CONTENTS.

LIST OF ILLUSTRATIONS.

"In the name of the Prophet — FIGS!"

THE SQUIBOB PAPERS.

I.

FOURTH OF JULY ORATION IN OREGON.

Correspondence.

"*Fort Vancouver, W. T., June* 15, 1856.

"JOHN PHŒNIX, Esq., Sergt. Major, etc.

"DEAR SIR: — I am requested by a number of your brother officers, and other gentlemen, to solicit you to deliver the oration at the celebration of the approaching Fourth of July, at this post.

"Very respectfully,

"Your friend and obdt. servt.,

"H. C. H.,

"1st Lieut 4th Infantry."

"*Portland, Oh! Tea, June,* 1856.

"DEAR SIR: — I have the honor to acknowledge the receipt of your very polite invitation to address a number of my brother officers, and other gentlemen, on the coming glorious anniversary, at Vancouver.

"In the words of a celebrated Roman emperor, when asked to take a drink, I reply, 'I will do it with great pleasure,' and shall immediately prepare myself for the discharge of the agreeable duty thus devolving upon me.

"Your invitation, Sir, arrived upon a most opportune occasion. Eighty years (or thereabouts) ago, this day, our respected ancestors marched up the side of Breed's Hill by a flank, to the following spirit-stirring tune:

'Oh! tweedle dum twee,
Oh! tweedle dum twee,
Oh! tweedle-tweedle, tweedle dum twee.'

And after getting there, feeling sick at their stomachs from fatigue, threw up a line of breastworks and trenches, that took the British very particularly by surprise. Behind those breastworks, sir, our gallant ancestors stood shoulder to shoulder, and received the red-coated minions of the British monarch with a galling and destructive fire, that caused them to retreat in confusion. Three successive times was the attack repeated, and three successive times were the British mercenaries repulsed. At the fourth attempt, Sir, our ancestors suddenly remembered certain business engagements in the country which could no longer be neglected, and they had not time to remain and see the matter through. They left; and a mingled mass of cowhide boots and shirt-tails fluttering in the distance, was all the British could descry, when, out of breath, perfectly exhausted, they arrived on the summit of Breed's. This great engagement, Sir, was named the battle of Bunker Hill, on account of its not having occurred on a hill of that name, and a monument two hundred feet high has been erected on the spot, from the top of which a man once fell, and knocked the whole top off of his derned eternal head, Sir!

"From the top of this monument now floats the

glorious spang-dangled stanner of our country, and long may it wave.

"Please, Sir, to accept the renewed assurances of the most distinguished consideration. *Carry and Stevens!*

"With singular respect, I remain

"Your most obdt. servt.,

"JOHN PHŒNIX.

"Lieut. H. SEA H.,
"1st. Lieut. 4th U. S. Foot
"Vancouver, W. Tea."

Oration:

DELIVERED AT FORT VANCOUVER W. T., ON THE FOURTH OF JULY, 1856, BY JOHN PHŒNIX, £ S. D., SERGEANT MAJOR, EIGHTY-THIRD REGIMENT, OREGON TERRITORY LIGHT MULES.

"BROTHER SOLDIERS AND FELLOW CITIZENS:—I feel honored by the call that I have received and accepted to deliver on this great occasion, the glorious anniversary of our nation's independence, the customary oration. The word oration signifying a public address, I have reason to believe has a mil itary origin. It originated in a custom once prevalent among commanding officers and chaplains, of making long and verbose addresses to the troops, which were stigmatized as 'all talk and no rations,' whence the word noration, modernized into oration. The term address has also a similar origin, it having been the custom for the troops to be dressed to the right before the oration was delivered. From the word noration is derived the common expression — common in the sweet and classic vales of Pike — 'to norate.' Thus we hear an individual wishing to refer to an anecdote related to him in early life by his grandmother, say, '*I hurd her norrate it.*'

"This explanation may appear irrelevant and uninteresting; but I never lose an opportunity to impart a little valuable information.

"Brother soldiers and fellow citizens: It is the Fourth of July. This morning, at half-past two o'clock, every inhabitant of this great, free, and enlightened republic, amounting in number to several millions, was awakened from a sleep by the discharge of cannon, the explosion of fire-crackers, and the continued and reïterated shouts of little boys, and children of larger growth. From that time until four o'clock sleep has been rendered impossible, and every inhabitant of this republic has had an opportunity to reflect with gratitude and thankfulness on the wisdom of our progenitors, and the greatness of our institutions; until at that hour the bells of every church, meeting-house, factory, steam-boat, and boarding-house throughout the land, beginning to pour forth a merry and universal peal, joining in the glad anthem of our nation's independence, every citizen has got up, put on his pantaloons, taken a cock-tail, and commenced the celebration of the day in good earnest.

"Throughout our whole vast extent of country, from Hancock Barracks, Houlton, Maine, where they pry the sun up in the morning, to Fort Yuma on the Colorado River, where the thermometer stands at 212° in the shade, and the hens lay hard hard-boiled eggs, this day will be a day of hilarity, of frolicking and rejoicing.

"Processions will be formed, churches will be thronged, orations will be delivered, (many of them, possibly, of a superior character to this of mine,) the gallant militia, that right arm of our national defence, will pervade the streets in astounding uniforms, whereof it may be said that Solomon in all his glory was *not* arrayed like one of these. Small boys will fire pistols and burn their fingers ; large boys will fire cannon and blow off their arms; men will guzzle inebriating liquors, and become much intoxicated thereby ; and a mighty shout will go up from the land, which, if the wind happens to be in the right direction, will cause the Emperor Alexander to tremble in his boots, and the young Napoleon to howl in his silver cradle. For on this day the great American eagle flaps her wings, and soars aloft, until it makes your eyes sore to look at her, and looking down upon her myriads of free and enlightened children, with flaming eye, she screams, '*E Pluribus Unum*,' which may be freely interpreted, 'Aint I some?' and myriads of freemen answer back with joyous shout: 'You *are* punkins!' On this glorious day, joy, good feeling, and good nature animate each breast; babies cease to cry, ladies cease to scold, all is amiability; and I hesitate not to say, that were the commanding general of this Division on this day to ask the Governor of Oregon for a chew of tobacco, he would hand over the whole plug without a moment's delay or hesitation. And what is the cause of this general rejoicing, this universal hilarity, this amiable state of feeling, this love and veneration for this particular day of all days in the year — a day when the native American forgets all prejudices, and, though loving his country better than aught else, feels well disposed toward every thing beside — a day that our German population respect and speak of as 'more better as good' — a day which Pat, who believes one man is as good as another, and a mighty sight better, reverences as he does 'Saint Patrick's in the morning' — a day when aught unpleasant is forgotten, and mirth, and jollity, and fire-crackers abound. I will endeavor to inform you. Many years ago, before Vancouver was ever born or thought of, when the present magnificent city of Portland was but a wild forest of fir timber, and the waters of these mighty rivers, now daily ploughed by the splendid steamer 'Eagle,' were navigated by the Indian chief Multnomah in his dug-out, provisioned with salmon and whortleberries, there dwelt in the far-off city of Genoa, a worthy merchant named Daniel Lumbus, who prosecuted his business as a dealer in velvets, under the name and style of Lumbus & Co.

"This merchant, at a somewhat advanced age, was blest with a son of great promise, whom, out of compliment to his partners, he named Christopher Co Lumbus. From his earliest infancy this youth showed an ardent desire for a maritime life; and old Lumbus gratified his inclinations by sending him to sea.

"In those days popular opinion turned to the belief that this world on which we live was a large square table, or plane surface, supported on columns of rocks, which extended all the way down.

Columbus, however, dissented from this opinion, and believing the earth to be a globe or ball, decided in his own mind that it might be feasible to start in a given direction, aud sail clear round it, returning to the point of departure. Having communicated these views to Isabella, the Qneen of Arragon, that lady, who was somewhat of an enthusiast, and had a srong conviction that Columbus was ' one of them," sold her hoop ear-rings and other jewelry, and fitted out three top-sail schooners, of which she gave him the command.

" With these vessels, Christopher sailed in 1492, and after the most unheard-of trials and difficulties, encountering many head-winds, and much opposition from his crew, finally discovered the West India Islands, whence he immediately returned with a cargo of rum and sugar. This extraordinary discovery being noised abroad, a Spanish captain, who from his jovial disposition was called A Merry Cuss, sailed away, and discovered this continent, which, from its discoverer, derived the name of America. Then New England was discovered by John Cabot, and Virginia by Walter Raleigh, who also discovered tobacco, and gave himself dyspepsia by smoking it to excess, and Pocahontas was discovered by John Smith, and South Carolina by Calhoun.

"Emigration from Great Britian and other countries then commenced, and continued to a tremendous extent, and all our fore-fathers, and eight grandfathers, came over and settled in the land.

"They planted corn and built houses, they killed the Indians, hung the Quakers and Baptists, burned the witches alive, and were very happy and comfortable indeed. So matters went on very happily, the colonies thus formed owing allegiance to the government of Great Britain until the latter part of the eighteenth century, when a slight change took place in their arrangements. The king of Great Britain, a Dutchman of the name of George Guelph, No. 3, having arrived at that stage of life when Dutchmen generally, if at all inclined that way, naturally begin to give way to ill-temper and obstinacy, became of a sudden exceedingly overbearing and ill-disposed toward the colonies. He had offenders sent to England to be tried; he was down on a bank and a protective tariff, and began to be considered little better than an abolitionist. He also put in effect an ordinance called the Stamp Act, which prevented applause in places of public amusement, prevented the protection of cattle against flies, and interfered with the manufacture of butter; and he finally capped the climax of his audacious impositions by placing such a tremendous duty on tea, that our female ancestors could not afford to drink that exhilarating beverage. Our ancestors were patient and long-suffering, but they could not stand every thing.

"Souchong and Young Hyson cost about twelve-and-a-half cents a cup; and our grandmothers were weeping with vexation, and would not be comforted with herb-tea and decoctions of sassafras. They annoyed our grandfathers to that extent that they rebelled, got up a Vigilance Committee in Boston, and destroyed two cargoes of English tea, and were fired on by the British troops in consequence. Then the whole country flew to arms; the battles of Concord and of Lexington followed, and our grandfathers went marching up to the tune of Yankee Doodle to the top of Bunker's Hill, whence they did not march down until they had given the British troops a most fearful and ever-to-be-remembered whipping. By this time it suddenly occurred to some of the smartest of our respectable ancestors that it was a good long way to the little island of England, that there was a good many people in the provinces, and that perhaps they were quite as able to govern themselves as George Guelph No. 3 was to govern them. They accordingly appointed delegates from the various Provinces or States, who, meeting together in Philadelphia on the fourth day of July, 1776, decided to trouble the King of England no longer, and gave to the world that glorious Declaration of Independence, to the support of which they pledged their lives, their fortunes, and their sacred honor. This was the birth-day of Freedom — the birth-day of the United States, now eighty years of age; and as there are few of us but feel some inclination to celebrate our own birth-day, there can be little wonder that we celebrate the birth-day of our country in so joyous, earnest, and enthusiastic a manner.

"Love of country is strongly impressed on every mind; but, as Americans, we should and in fact do have this feeling more strongly developed than any other citizens of the world. For our country is a free country; its institutions are wise and liberal, and our advantages as its natives are greater than those of other citizens. To be sure, every body can vote two or three times in some places; it is true taxes are four and a half per cent on the amount of our property; it's a fact that it's difficult to get scrip paid; there's no disputing the existence of the Maine Liquor Law; and we do occasionally have a mob; but these are errors not arising from the principles of our government, but from circumstances, and they will finally obviate and correct themselves. Upon the whole, I believe that a man has quite as much chance for a life of happiness if born under the glorious stars and stripes as if he happened to be born anywhere else, and perhaps a little more. We elect our own rulers, and make our own laws, and if they don't turn out well, it's very easy at the next election to make others in their place. Every body has a chance for distinction in this country; nothing is wanting but natural ability to attain it; and Mrs. Laving Pike's baby, now lying with a cotton-flannel shirt on, in a champagne basket, in Portland, O. T., has just as good a chance of being president of the United States, as the imperial infant of France, now sucking his royal thumbs in his silver cradle at Paris, has of being an emperor. I do not wish to flatter this audience; I do not intend to be thought particularly complimentary; but I do assure you, that there is not a man present who, if he had votes enough, might not be elected president of the United States. And this important fact is the result not so much of any particular merit or virtue on your part, as of the nature of our glorious, liberal, republican institutions.

" In this great and desirable country, any man may become rich, provided he will make money; and man may be well educated, if he will learn, and has money to pay for his board and schooling; and any man may become great, and of weight in the community, if he will take care of his health, and eat sufficiently of boiled salmon and potatoes.

" Moreover, I assert it unblushingly, any man in this country may marry any woman he pleases — the only difficulty being for him to find any woman that he does please.

" Fellow-citizens and brother soldiers: It is the Fourth of July; it is Independence Day — a day dear to every freeman, an anniversary which is good to celebrate, as it will be celebrated till time shall cease, and the Union shall perish with it.

" Every boy in these United States knows the origin of this glorious day. Small sums of money, varying from twelve-and-a-half cents to a dollar and a half, according to the financial prosperity of their parents, have been annually given them to expend on this occasion, which indelibly impress the fact upon their memories, and lead them to look forward with pleasure to its return. One of my earliest and most cherished recollections is of my exploits on the first Fourth of July that I can remember, when, with patriotic fervor, I purchased a leaden cannon, which, exploding prematurely, burned off my hair and eye-brows, and put an end to the existence of a favorite cat of my aunt's that peacefully reclined, watching my operations. It is considered by many a duty to become intoxicated on the Fourth of July. I remember hearing a distinguished Senator express his opinion, 'that any man who did not get drunk on the Fourth of July was a damned rascal.' Without fully coinciding in this novel hypothesis, I can truly say, that I consider it the duty of every freeman to enjoy himself to the full limits of his capacity on this glorious occasion, and if there are, as I dare say there are, individuals to whom getting drunk is the acme of human felicity, why, if they do allow themselves to be carried away on this day, there is surely more excuse for them than there would be on any less joyous occasion. An anecdote that went the round of the papers a few years since is amusing and interesting, as showing the independent feeling engendered in the minds of all classes by the arrival of the glorious Fourth.

"A parsimonious merchant who, I regret to say, flourished in Boston, kept his counting-room open on Independence Day, where he sat with his clerk, a boy of ten or twelve years of age, busy over his accounts, while the noise and uproar of the celebration were resounding without. Looking up from his employment, he perceived the unfortunate youth, perched upon his high stool, engaged in picking his nose, a practice that the merchant had frequently reprobated, and taken him to task for.

"'William,' he exclaimed, 'why will you persist in that dirty practice? I am astonished at you.'

"'I don't care,' whimpered the unhappy boy. 'It's Independence day, and it's my own nose, and I'll pick thunder out of it.'

"An excellent custom prevails in many cities of the United States to celebrate the close of this day with a grand exhibition of fire-works. This is not only a beautiful and exciting spectacle, but, to the thinking mind, presents a refined pleasure in the analogy that is suggested; for he may think to himself that, as the day ends, so will end the lives of the enemies of freedom and the incendiary abolitionists, who threaten with parricidal efforts the union of these States. They will be followed by a grand display of fire-works in another world, if there is any truth in the orthodox doctrines of the age. I have never known a Fourth of July oration delivered, and I have listened to many, without a full and complete biography of the immortal Washington being given before its conclusion. It may appear a slightly hackneyed custom, but I shall certainly not let you go off without it. At the risk of appearing tedious, I shall therefore request your patience for a few moments, while I read from the 'Clatrap Cyclopedia,' by Professor Tube Rose, the following beautiful tribute to the memory of this greatest of men:

[FROM TUBE ROSE'S AMERICAN BIOGRAPHY.]

"'GENERAL GEORGE WASHINGTON.

"George Washington was one of the most distinguished movers in the American Revolution.

"He was born of poor but honest parents, at Genoa, in the year 1492. His mother was called the mother of Washington. He married, early in life, a widow lady, Mrs. Martha Custis, whom Prescott describes as the *cussidest* pretty woman south of Mason and Dixon's line. Young Washington commenced business as a county-surveyor, and was present in that character at a sham fight, under General Braddock, when so many guns were fired that the whole body of militia were stunned by the explosion, and sate down to supper unable to hear a word that was said. This supper was afterward alluded to as Braddock's deaf eat, and the simile, 'deaf as a Braddock,' subsequently vulgarized into 'deaf as a haddock,' had its rise from that circumstance. Washington commanded several troops during the Revolutionary war, and distinguished himself by fearlessly crossing the Delaware river on ice of very inadequate thickness, to visit a family of Hessians of his acquaintance. He was passionately fond of green peas and string beans; and his favorite motto was: 'In time of peace prepare for war.'

"Washington's most intimate friend was a French gentleman, named Marcus Dee, who, from his constant habits of risibility, was nick-named '*Laughy yet.*' His greatest victory was achieved at Germantown, where, coming upon the British in the night, he completely surrounded them with a wall of cotton bales, from which he opened a destructive and terrific fire, which soon caused the enemy to capitulate. The cotton bales being perforated with musket-balls were much increased in weight, and consequently in value, and the expression, playfully used, 'What is the price of cotton?' was much in vogue after the battle.

"During the action, Washington might have been seen driving up and down the lines, exposed to a deadly fire, in a small Concord wagon, drawn by a bob-tailed gray horse. His celebrated dispatch, '*Veni, vidi, vici,*' or, I came and saw in a Concord wagon, has reference to this circumstance.

"Washington has been called the 'Father of his country;' (an unapt title, more properly belonging to the late Mr. McCluskey, parent of the celebrated pugilist;) the child has grown, however, to that extent that its own father would not know it. General Walker (William Walker) is also called the 'Father of Nicaragua,' and we have no doubt, in case of his demise, his children, the native Nicaraguans, would erect a suitable monument over his remains, with the inscription, 'Go, father, and fare worse.'

"Washington was a member of the Know-

Nothing order, and directed that none but Americans should be put on guard, which greatly annoyed the Americans, their comfort being entirely destroyed by perpetual turns of guard-duty.

"He was twice elected President of the United States by the combined Whig and Know-Nothing parties, the Democrats and Abolitionists voting against him; and served out his time with great credit to himself and the country — drawing his salary with a regularity and precision worthy all commendation.

"Although, for the time in which he lived, a very distinguished man, the ignorance of Washington is something perfectly incredible. He never travelled on a steam-boat; never saw a railroad, or a locomotive engine; was perfectly ignorant of the principle of the magic of the magnetic telegraph; never had a daguerreotype, Colt's pistol, Sharp's rifle, or used a friction match. He eat his meals with an iron fork, never used postage-stamps on his letters, and knew nothing of the application of chloroform to alleviate suffering, or the use of gas for illumination. Such a man as this could hardly be elected president of the United States in these times, although, it must be confessed, we occasionally have a candidate who proves not much better informed about matters in general.

"Washington died from exposure on the summit of Mount Vernon, in the year 1786, leaving behind him a name that will endure forever, if posterity persist in calling their children after him to the same extent that has been fashionable. He is mentioned in history as having been 'first in peace, first in war, and first in the hearts of his countrymen;' in other words, he was No. 1 in every thing, and it was equally his interest and his pleasure to look out for that number, and he took precious good care to do so. A portrait, by Gilbert Stuart, of this great soldier and statesman may be seen, very badly engraved, on the 'History of the United States;' but as it was taken when the general was in the act of chewing tobacco, the left cheek is distended out of proportion,

(*See Frontispiece.*)

and the likeness rendered very unsatisfactory. Upon the whole, General George Washington was a very excellent man; though unfamiliar with 'Scott's Infantry Tactics,' he was a tolerable officer; though he married a widow, he was a fond husband; and though he did not know the Beecher family, (and would have despised them if he had,) he was a sincere Christian.

"E PLURIBUS UNUM.

"A monument has been commenced in the city of Washington to his memory, which is to be five hundred feet in height; and it should be the wish of every true-hearted American that his virtues and services may not be forgotten before it is completed; in which case, their remembrance will probably endure forever.

"Accustomed as I am to public speaking, it has been with no ordinary distrust of my own powers that I have ventured to address you to-day. Standing beneath the waving banner of our country, with Mount Hood towering in snow-crowned magnificence above our heads, and the broad bosom of the noble Columbia spread in calm expanse at our feet, I see before me an attentive audience composed of individuals whose interest I am proud to awaken and command. I see before me some who have borne no undistinguished part in the bloody but most righteous war now raging in our vicinity; I see men who have pushed the war into the enemy's country with the gallant Haller, and returned with him when he thought, perhaps, it would be about as well to leave; who accompanied the daring and skilful Raines, when intrepidly rushing with drawn sword at the head of his troops into Father Pandosy's hut, he wrote that letter to the humbled Kamiakin; men who have planned and built block-houses, which serve alike as refuges from the attacks of the savage and merciless foe, and imperishable monuments of architectural taste and refinement. These services, which have brought this war so nearly to a close, (for already the Sun of peace may be seen gilding the clouds in the east preparatory to rising,) are well worthy of commendation; and no better occasion can be found to recapitulate and commemorate them than the present.

"Where are the gallant volunteers on this occasion, our tried and trusty comrades in the hour of danger — men who, at the call of their country, cast aside the frivolous axe, the enervating hoe, and the trifling pick, and, springing into their eighty-dollar saddles, shouldered their fifty-dollar rifles, and spurred their three-hundred dollar horses into the wild plains of the Walla Walla, and there desperately and recklessly encamped? To what destruction were many of these daring spirits exposed, forced by the attacks of famine and the scarcity of fresh beef to live for weeks together on hard bread and pickled pork? They might yet have kept together had the whiskey still held out; but alas! like the early cloud and the morning dew, it passed away, and even the jar that contained the ears of P. P. Mox Mox was exhausted! Then they returned — slowly and sadly they returned — and those who had never been peppered in service were mustered out. Like the prophets of old, they went forth with their staff and their scrip; but the staff soon resigned their commissions, and the scrip has not yet been paid. But, by the blessing of Heaven and Saint Pike, that consummation, so devoutly to be wished, will yet be arrived at. The scrip will be paid, and we shall see Pike flourishing like a green bay horse.

"The toils and dangers of the war will be forgotten; in the elegant luxury and refinement of their homes, hardships will be looked back upon with pleasure; the physical suffering and results of exposure will yield to skilful treatment, and those who have suffered from sleeping on hard beds in the wilderness, can now console themselves by lying on wool.

"In future times, when by some impartial historian the present Oregon war is faithfully depicted, posterity, as it peruses the volume, will drop a tear o'er the picture of the sufferings of those noble volunteers that wallowed in the Walla Walla valley, and their intrepid march into that country, and their return, will excite a thrill of admiration as an adventure never equaled even by Napoleon H. Bonaparte, when he effected the passage of the Alps.

But the war will soon be ended; it is even now drawing to a close. The completion of the Pacific railroad, which may be looked upon as certain in the course of the next fifty years, increasing our facilities for transportation of arms and supplies, will undoubtedly have a most favorable effect; and I look upon it as a matter of little doubt that, three or four hundred years from this time, hostilities will have ceased entirely, and the Indians will have been liberally treated with, and become quiet and valuable members of our society.

The influence of that glorious banner will have been felt by them; they will have been made to see stars; they will have been compelled to feel stripes; and all will be peace and harmony, love and joy among them. Four hundred, years from this time, the descendants of Kamiakin will be celebrating with our posterity the recurrences of this glorious day, with feelings of interest and delight. While to-day that great chief, moved by feelings of animosity toward us, sits and gnaws the gambrel-joint of a defunct Cayuga pony, little knowing on which side of his staff of life the oleaginous product of lactation is disseminated. But long after that time shall arrive, centuries and centuries after our difficulties shall have been settled, and the scrip, with accumulated interest, paid, may our glorious institutions continue to flourish, may the Union be perpetuated forever in perfect bonds of strength and faternal affection, and the

"Star-spangled banner continue to wave
O'er the land of the free and the home of the brave."

MUSIC BY THE BAND.

II.

A CALIFORNIA "MODEL LOVE-LETTER."

Mariesville july fore 1856.

DEAR CATE, you know I luv you mor an any uther Girle in the World, and wat's the Reson you allways want Me to tell you so. I no you ar almost gitting tired of waiting for me; I no you luv me fit to brake your hart. I no we ort to git marid, but how kin we if we kant — sa! Wat's the use in thinkin bout it. I thort wen I sold mi mule that I wud have nough to pay the precher and by you nice goun. But I tried mi luk at poker and got strapt the fust nite. Cate, you never played poker — in korse not. Wel, it's a confounded mity nice game as long as you kin sit behind a smorl par; but when you kant get a par, the pot's gone. I luv you so much, Cate, that I allmost hav a notion to sel me 1 horse wagin and buck a nite or 2 at farow; but how kin I — sa!

Mi whol wagin wudent fech more an fore or 5 good staks. ile go baek to the mountings an work and dig and swet and do every thing I kin to get money to git marid. I ain't any ways gelus, Cate, but pleze don't hug and kiss and set on J——n B——s lapp any noor. you know he ain't worth shaks, he kant drink mor an 3 hornes 'thout gittin tite; I kin stand up under fiftey. You know I kin liek him 2, and hav dun it and kin do it agin. But I ain't a bit gelus, I no I out to marid long ago. leven years is rether long to kort a gal, but ile hav you yit Cate.

Good by, till next we meet.

Your affeckunate Lover,

D—— G——.

Note a bena, good-by agin. Run that feller off.

2th P. S. I'm nat a bit gelus, Cate; but don't let him cum bout the house.

LEFTENANT CARTER AND HIS SON.—*See page* 45.

I.

ON Springfield Mounting, thar did dwell
A likely youth, I knowed him well;
Leftenant Carter's only son,
A comely youth, nigh twenty-one.

II.

ONE Monday mornin, he did go,
Intew the meadow for to mow;
And all ter once, he thar did feel
A pizen sarpent bite his heel.

THE PIZEN SARPENT.—*See page* 46.

VENGEANCE, SWIFT AND SURE.—*See page* 47.

III.

QUICK as he felt the sarpent bite
He raised his scythe, with all his might
He struck ter once a deadly blow,
That laid the pizen creeter low.

IV.

HE tuk the riptyle in his hand,
And straight he went tew Molly Bland;
Oh! Molly, Molly, here you see
A pizen sarpent, what bit me.

The Grief of Molly Bland.—*See page 48.*

ZERUBBABEL IN TEARS.—*See page* 49.

V.

ZERUBBABEL, why did ye go,
Intu the meadow for to mow?
Oh! Molly Bland, I thought you knowed
'Twas Daddy's field, and must be mowed.

VI.

THEN Molly Bland, she squatted down,
And sucked the pizen from the wound;
But oh! she had a rotten tewth:
The venim soon affected both.

THE STRICKEN FAMILY.—*See page* 50.

THE LAST SAD RITES.—*See page* 51.

VII.

OH, then they ware all spotted o'er
With all the colors that the sarpent wore,
They laid 'em both upon a bed,
And they swelled up and di-i-ed!

VIII.

THEN when they had gin up the ghost,
From "Springfield Mounting" they went post;
And they larfed, and sung, as up they went,
As chipper, as if there wa'nt no pizen Sar-*pent*.

EXIT ZERUBBABEL AND MOLLY BLAND.—*See page* 52.

IV.

PHŒNIX ON AGRICULTURE.

San Francisco, Feb'y 7, 1856.

Col. J. L. Warren, Sec. Cal. State Ag. Society :

My Dear Sir : I have the honor to acknowledge the receipt, this day, of your very polite and flattering invitation (dated Aug. 25, 1855,) to deliver a poem of my own composition before the Annual meeting of the State Agricultural Society, in September last. Though somewhat diffident regarding my powers in the poetical line, (feeling in fact very much like the Irishman immortalized by Miller, who when asked if he could play upon the fiddle, replied that "he presumed he could, 'though he had never tried,") I shall accept the invitation, and shall endeavor to discharge the duty devolving upon me to the best of my ability. You do me more than justice in supposing that I take a strong interest in the newly developed resources of our glorious State, in an agricultural point of view; and I have in fact, as you may be aware, devoted some little time to the pleasing science of horticulture in my endeavors to show up the greens of California.

I see nothing to regret in the arrival of your invitation, it gives me sufficient time to prepare, and I doubt not, that by the return of last September I shall be able to present to the Society a poem that will be among poems, what Niagara is among cataracts, or Oregon among civilized nations.

I already begin to feel a grand agricultural, floral horticultural, and pomological poetic fervor stealing over me, under the influence of which, I have without much effort composed the following admirable lines as a beginning:

Here's to the land of potatoes and carrots,
Whose banks grow wild, rich bacon and parrots;
Where each apple and pear a dollar apiece is,
And a man may devour just as much as he pleases;
(*Spoken — If he's the money to pay for them.*)
Where the soil is teeming with vegetable treasures,
And a pumpkin ten feet in circumference measures;
Where to root up a turnip, an ox team employed is;

By each laborer a very large salary enjoyed is;
(*Play on the word celery.*)
And kind Colonel Warren, with interest watches
The growth of his parsley and marrowfat squashes,
And stirs up the farmers, and gives them rules of action, and incentives to exertion, and constantly teaches,
How they ought not to let Oregon get ahead of them, but establish nurseries at once where they could raise at very trifling expense, all kinds of grafted fruit, pears and apples, and cherries and the most delicious peaches, &c., &c., &c.

That last line seems a little exuberant, probably it results from the rich nature of the soil, but there is plenty of time to apply the pruning knife. Thanking you heartily for your kindness and presenting my compliments to the Society, to whom I beg you will communicate my acceptance of their polite invitation,

I remain,

With great respect and esteem

Your friend and ob't serv't.

SQUIBOB.

V.

NEVER TOLD A LIE.

SMALL Joe L—— was playing one sunny morning in a yard at the rear of his residence, when essaying to cast a stone high in air, he found he had miscalculated his strength, or the weight of the stone, as that missile slipped from his fingers, and taking an entirely different direction from that intended, went whack through a pane of glass in the neighbor's window. Mrs. Connolly, who was engaged in washing in the kitchen, hearing the smash of glass in her spare room, rushed hastily to the scene of action, and through the broken pane beheld Joe in active retreat. Irate and indignant, the injured matron sought the presence of Mrs. L——, and straight poured forth the story of her wrongs. Mrs. L—— assumed a dignified air; the culprit was called to "the presence;"

and the inquest on the departed pane commenced. "Joseph," said Mrs. L——, with awful solemnity, "did you break the glass in Mrs. Connolly's window?" "Yes'm," replied Joe with promptitude. "Joseph," said Mrs. L——, "if you broke that pane of glass, I shall certainly correct you: did you break it, Sir?" Joe hesitated, but conscience was powerful, and he replied that he did. Mrs. L—— took a stick from the mantel-piece: "Joseph," said she, "if you broke that glass I shall correct you most severely: I ask again, did you break it?" Joe looked at his mother; he looked at the stick; and hanging his head, he murmured: "No ma'am." "*There!*" said Mrs. L——, triumphantly, "that boy never told me a lie in his life. I *know'd* he never broke no window; 'spect your little Guster broke it; she hove a stone clear over our fence yesterday." That's a good style of encouraging truthfulness in a child, "we *don't* think!"

VI.

SEWING MACHINE — FELINE ATTACHMENT.

CIRCULAR: TO THE PUBLIC.

PERMIT me to call your undivided attention to an invention lately made and patented by myself, which is calculated to produce the most beneficial results, and prove of inestimable value to mankind. It is well known that the sewing-machines now so generally in use, are the most important invention and greatest blessing of the age. Every lady considers this instrument indispensable to her happiness; it has completely usurped the place of the piano-forte and harp in all well-regulated families; and she who once purchased materials for clothing by the yard, now procure them by the piece or bolt to enjoy the rational pleasure of easily making them into garments.

In the humble cabin of the laborer, and in the halls of the rich and great, now resounds from morning until night, the whir of the sewing-machine. The result of this universal grinding, although eminently gratifying to the sellers of dry goods, and the philanthropic fathers and husbands who discharge their bills, has not been of a favorable nature to our ladies in a physical point of view. It is found that the constant use of the crank has brought on rheumatic and neuralgic affections in the shoulder, and a similar application of the treddle has a tendency to produce hip diseases, and white swelling of the knee-joint, accompanied by nervous complaints of a painful character. The undersigned is acquainted with a most estimable single lady of middle age, who, having procured one of the fast-running machines, was so enchanted with it, that she persisted in its use for thirty-six hours without cessation, and found, on endeavoring to leave off, that her right leg had acquired the motion of the treddle in such a painful manner, that it was impossible to keep it still, and her locomotion therefore assumed a species of polka step exceedingly ludicrous to witness, and particularly mortifying to herself. I regret to add that she was compelled, by a vote of the society, to withdraw from the Methodist Church, on a charge of dancing down the broad aisle on a Communion Sunday. A more melancholy instance was the case of Mrs. Thompson of Seekonk, a most amiable lady, beloved and respected by all around her, but who, by constant use of the crank, lost all control of the flexors and extensors of her right arm, and inadvertently punched her husband in the eye, which, he being a man of suspicious and unforgiving disposition, led to great unhappiness in the family, and finally resulted in the melancholy case of Thompson *vs.* Thompson, so familiar to most of the civilized world. A turn for mechanism, and an intense desire to contribute to the happiness of the female sex, have ever been distinguishing traits in my character. On learning these facts, therefore, I devoted myself to a thorough investigation of the subject, and after a month of close application, have at last made an invention which will at once do away with every thing objectionable in the use of the sewing-machine.

This beautiful discovery is now named

"PHŒNIX'S FELINE ATTACHMENT."

Like most great inventions, the Attachment is of great simplicity. An upright shaft is connected with the machine by a cog-wheel and pinion, and supported below by a suitable frame-work. Two projecting arms are attached to the shaft, to one of which a large cat is connected by a light harness, and from the other, a living mouse is suspended by the tail, within a few inches of the nose of the *motor*. As the cat springs toward the mouse, the latter is removed, and keeping constantly at the original distance, the machine revolves with great rapidity. The prodigious velocity produced by the rapacity of the cat in its futile endeavors to overtake the mouse, can only be imagined by one who has seen the Attachment in full operation.

It is thus that man shows his supremacy over the brute creation, by making even their rapacious instincts subservient to his use.

Should it be required to arrest the motion of the machine, a handkerchief is thrown over the mouse, and the cat at once pauses, disgusted.

Remove the handkerchief and again she springs forward with renewed ardor. The writer has seen one cat (a tortoise-shell) of so ardent and unwearying disposition, that she made eighteen pairs of men's pantaloons, two dozen shirts, and seven stitched shirts, before she lay down exhausted. It is to be hoped that the ladies throughout the land will avail themselves of this beautiful discovery, which will entirely supersede the use of the needle, and make the manufacture of clothing and household materials a matter of pleasure to themselves, and exciting and healthy exercise to their domestic animals. I present on page 63 an elevation of the " Feline Attachment " in operation, that all may understand its powers, and none fail to procure one, through ignorance of its merits.

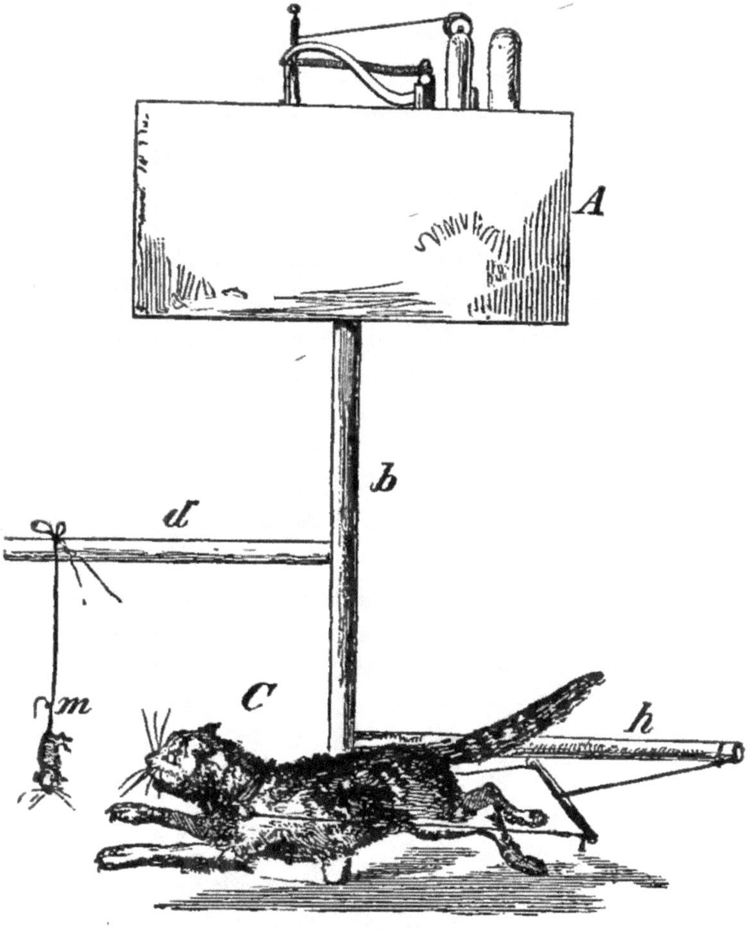

ELEVATION OF 'PHŒNIX'S FELINE ATTACHMENT.'

A. Sewing-Machine, Box-pattern, ...	$75 00
C. Cat, at various prices, say, ...	$2½ to 10 00
B. Vertical Shaft, ...	5 00
D. H. Projecting arms, ...	50
M. Mouse, ...	12½
Total cost of Machine and Attachment, ...	$90 62½

The Attachment will be furnished to families having sewing-machines, on the most reasonable terms, and at the shortest notice. Young and docile cats supplied with the Attachment, by application at 348 Broadway, New York. Office of the Patent Back-Action Hen Persuader.

VII.

PHŒNIX ON WET WEATHER.

Portland Oregon T. August

IT gives me unfeigned pleasure to inform you that I am about to quit the gloomy and never-to-be-dried-up sky of Oregon, and "repair without unnecessary delay" to D———, on our borders. Yes, Sir, I'm off; "services" no longer required on these inclement shores — shores, which, when you read of in Irving's "Astoria," you naturally wish to behold, and admire old Astor's pluck in making establishments thereon, and which, when you reach, you wish you hadn't, and admire still more old Astor's good sense in breaking his establishments up, and quitting while there was yet time.

Rain is an exceedingly pleasant and gratifying

institution in its way, and in moderation ; it causes the grass to grow, the blossoms to flourish, and is a positive necessity to the umbrella-maker ; but when you get to a country where it rains incessantly twenty-six hours a day, for seventeen months in the year, you cannot resist having the conviction forced upon your mind that the thing is slightly overdone. That's the case in Oregon ; it commenced raining pretty heavily on the third of last November, and continued up to the fifteenth of May, when it set in for a long storm, which isn't fairly over yet. There's moisture for you.

The consequences of this awful climate are just what might be supposed. The immense quantity of the protoxide squirted about here causes trees, buildings, streets, every thing, to present a diluted and wishy-washy appearance. The women lose their color, the men their hair, (washed off, Sir,) and the animals, by constant exposure, acquire scales and fins, like the natives of the great deep. In fact, all the inhabitants of this territory have a generally scaly appearance, and rejoice in a peculiar smell, a combination, I should say, of a fish-ball and a fresh mud-sucker. The rains of Oregon beat every thing in that line I ever beheld or conceived of. Those that fell on Noah's ark were not more heavy; those of Nero, Caligula, and I. Neely Johnson, not more terrible; nor those of Lady Suffolk and Moscow longer or stronger, which is a slightly mixed metaphor of a very happy description. So, upon the whole, I'm glad I'm off; yes, I am quite sure of it; and I long to get to D——, where the people enjoy the light of the blessed sun, and where I can enjoy it also, and dry my things, and read Irving's "Astoria."

Howbeit, there are many interesting and curious things in Oregon; many odd and entertaining people also therein; and I have seen much that was funny, and laughed thereat, and should have laughed louder and longer if my mouth had not filled with rain before I had half finished; and I might perhaps regret leaving a country in which I have had so much positive enjoyment, were it not that I have chronicled all these amusing things and peculiarities, and shall be glad to get somewhere where I can have a dry laugh over them. Such a thing as "dry humor" in Oregon is, of course, a physical impossibility.

A slight history of the Oregon war, with some incidents from the life of Pike, is now in course of preparation, which, when finished, I will submit to you, with the hope that it may prove entertaining and improving to your readers. The information, certainly, is valuable, whatever may be the style. I inclose a short "Pome," which tells its own story. Set to music, ("suthin slow, and melancholy-like,") and accompanied by the *swinette*, I should think it might be well adapted for the parlor, the *boudoir*, or the concert-room. It is a plain, unvarnished tale, not only founded on facts, but with all three stories, and the attic, built of those materials.

STANZAS: LINES: SONG: BALLAD.

"Among them that came up to speculate in stock and supplies."

A OREGON LAY.

BY A SURVIVING SUFFERER OF THE WAR.

I.

Among them that come up to speculate in stock and supplies
Was a fellow named Stuart, a man of enterprise;
He bought him a switch-tail sorrel two-year old, which hed a white face,
And he bantered all Portland, O. T., for a three-hundred yard race.

II.

Thar was a man hed a horse, which he thought her pretty fair,
She was ginerally know'd as Millard's thousand-dollar mare;
He hadn't no idea, he said, of doing any thing so rash,
But he took up Mister Stuart for two hundred dollars, cash.

III.

So every soul in Portland, O. T., went straight down to the course,
And every cent we borryed, we bet on Millard's horse;
And thar was that speckilating Stuart, with his hand upon his hip,
And two men a-following with a tin pail full of dollars and a champagne-basket full of scrip!

IV.

Wal, they measured off the ground, and the horses got a start,
And came running down right pretty, about four foot apart;

And the Millard mare had it all her own way, so every body
said,
Till just as they got to the eend of the track, that are Sorrel
shot suthin' like ten feet ahead!

V.

Arter we seen that there riz a most surprising din,
And remarks like this ere followed, "Dog my everlastin skin,"
"I'll be dod-derned, and dog-gorned, and ding-blamed by
Pike,"
And thar was such awful howling, and swearing, *and* dancing,
that many old people said they never had seed the like.

VI.

And that are speckilatin Stuart, he made matters worse;
He packed the money into a hand-cart, and did'nt care a cuss,
And sweetly smiling, pulled it off, as though he didn't mind
the heft,
And since then we haint paid no taxes, nor bought nothing,
nor sold nothing, for I do suppose that in all Portland, O. T.,
there aint a single red cent left.

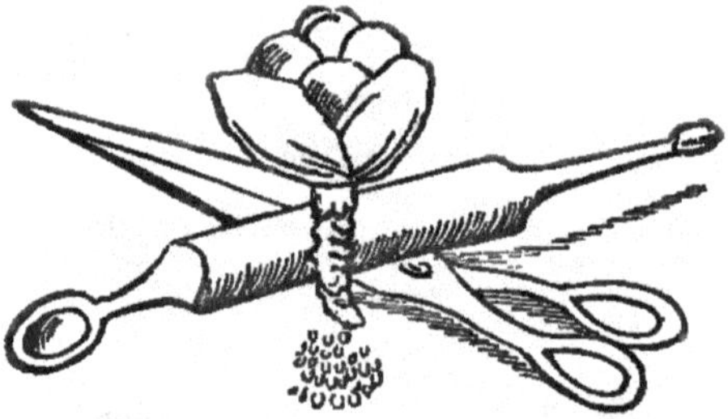

YE WARRE-LYKE BALLADE

OF YE

ASTOUNDEDDE

DOCTOR,

BY

PHENIX J. SQUIBOB

I.

IT was a fatte younge officer,
Who to a tayloure, came,
Tayloure! I would that thoue should'st make,
The garments that I name;
As quicklye as thoue mayeste
By either hooke or crooke,
And when they are completedde
Then charge them in thye booke.

4

II.

A COATE of brighte blue broadclothe,
With buttons alle of gilte,
A sashe of crimsone net worke,
And a sworde with brazen hilte,
A veste of snowe white dimitye,
And one of the colour of cream,
And a paire of broadclothe breeches,
With a stripe on the outer seame.

III.

THEN quickly seizing on his shears,
That tayloure did obey,
And ye garments, called for fashioned he,
In a quainte and curious waye,
In a harde knot he twined hys legges,
And to himself he said,
"I wonder, oh, I wonder,
If ever I'll be paid!"

IV.

TO ye Taylours's shop so gallantyle,
Ye officer did come ;
He clapped ye coate upon his backe
As ye Tayloure named ye sum.
Then sweetly thanked ye Tayloure,
For making him ye clothes,
And marched off, wagging pleasantlie
Hys fingers on hys nose.

TAYLOUR

V.

A YEAR soon passed, and all that time,
    Ye Tayloure never hearde
From that fatte younge officer, hys pen,
    Or otherwise a word;
He layed his shears upon his benche,
    Hys goose upon a coate,
And with hys leggs all tangled up
    He wrote him off a note.

VI.

"HOW now! oh, fatte younge officer!"
Thus the tayloure he did say,
"For your raiment that I furnished,
Do you never mean to pay?
Now quickly send ye moneys
For all that I did make,
Or something awful I will do
To make ye Earthe to quake."

VII.

THEN laughed ye fatte younge officer
At ye Tayloure hys queer scrawl,
And though it was annoying
Was not annoyed at all.
No moneys had he, and he told
Ye Tayloure hys sad state,
In a letter which he wrote to him
"All for to *irritate*."

VIII.

THEN wrathfulle waxed ye Tayloure,
    And quickly he did send
To a high-born ladye who lived neare,
    Who was his dearest friend;
And while with rage hys knees they smote,
    And countenance turned pale,
He excited all her sympathy
    By hys interesting tayle.

IX.

TO her Lord, a learned Doctore,
Ye high-born ladye came;
" Now by my faith and halidome "
She cried, " It is foul shame."
Then the fat man's audacity
To him she did bewail,
And their tears flowed together o'er
The mournful taylour's tayle.

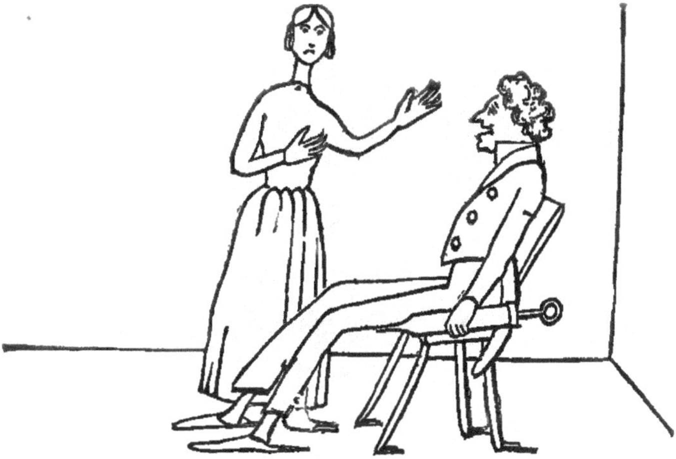

X.

NOW ye Doctor was a wise man,
Of exceeding great renown,
So he got him in hys buggye,
And posted up to town.
To all that officer, hys friends,
He quicklye spread ye news,
How fearfully that fleshy one,
Ye tayloure did abuse.

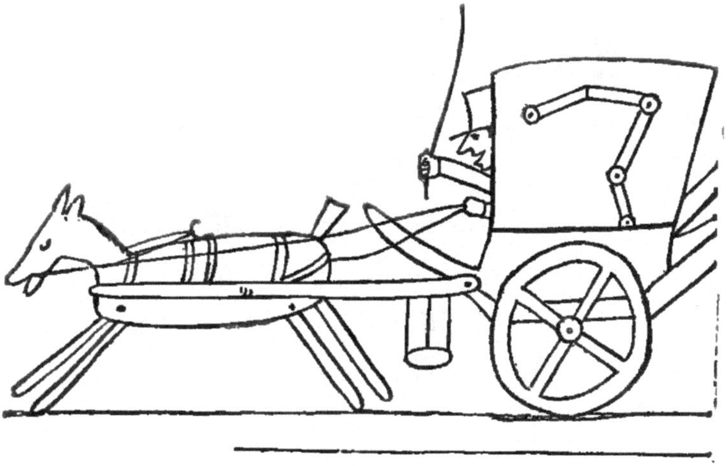

XI.

BUT ye Tayloure got hys moneys,
And then sayed, to be sure
He'd been as Taylours sometimes are,
A little premature.
So he wrote to ye young officer,
And gave hym great applause,
And he sayed he was a gentleman—
He always knowed he was.

XII.

BUT this moved not ye Doctor,
  Whose ideas being few,
When that he had got hold of one,
  Was bound to put it through.
So in a friendly manner,
  He still did circulate
The storye of ye letter,
  That was wrote to irritate.

XIII.

BUT ye aunt of ye younge officer,
She was a warre-lyke mayde,
And she sharpened up her finger-nayles,
Aud to his mother sayd,
" It is our determination
Straight to prepare for war ;
So up ye guards and at 'em,
We'll fix this old Doctor."

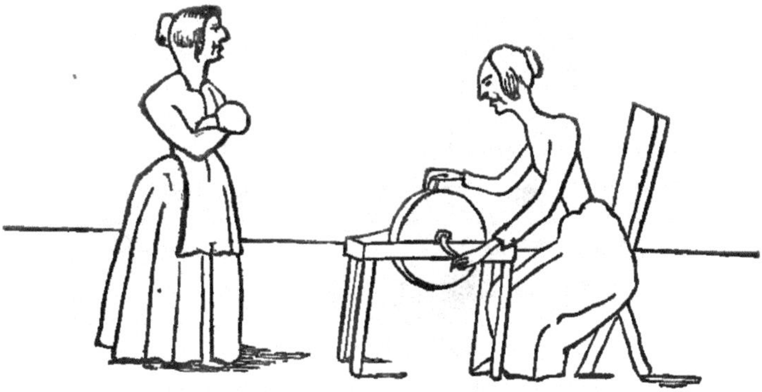

XIV.

BEHOLD them then, these fearless ones,
    Ye mother and ye mayde,
How gallantly against ye foe,
    Ye fat one they "arrayed."
Upon his belt they hung hys sword,
    And so they marched him round,
All which warre-lyke preparations
    Ye Doctor did "astound."

XV.

YE Doctor was "astoundedde,"
He wrote and told him so,
And sayed "if fyghtynge was their game,
With hym it was no go;
He had bled for hys countrye,
In fact had blystered too,
But with feuds of this description
He would nothing have to do."

XVI.

HERE'S a health to ye, Doctor.
    Ye Tayloure and hys friend,
And whatsoe'er they undertake
    May full success attend.
Goose, syringe, shears and press-board
    Doses, draughts and pills,
Cabbage and cathartics,
    Scissors, lancet, buckram, BILLS.

IX.

LIFE IN PANAMA.

SCENE. — The interior of one of our principal hotels. — GEN. PLATES, the "spirited proprietor is discovered sitting behind his bar, engaged in the pleasing occupation of estimating the profits of the day, and reflecting on his "sacred honor." A long table is seen in an adjoining apartment, covered with dirty sheets, and lavishly spread with dark boiled rice, jerked beef, hard bread and the other delicacies of the season. Deep groans are heard at intervals from the two hundred and forty famished boarders, imprisoned and partially smothering in squads of five in small pens, six feet by eight. A decidedly unwholesome effluvia pervades the entire building.

GEN. PLATES (*reflectively*). — Two hundred and forty boarders, at two dollars a day, is, let me see, twice oughts an ought, and — four hundred and eighty dollars, from which take for expenses, say five dollars, leaves a clear profit of——

(*Enter* DODGE, BLATHERSKITE, FLATBROKE *and others.*)

DODGE.— Well, General, the steamer *are* here, and *me* and the boys *is* bound to go. Now, we've been a living with you for two weeks, and what with the derned monte banks and other extravagances, we're completely busted, and havn't a red to pay our bills with.

GEN. PLATES. — Why, d——n your impudence, ——

BLATHERSKITE, — Oh, dry up, General. Here, just take a look at this here, [*Hands a document to Plates, who reads aloud :*]

TO THE PUBLIC.

CITY OF PANAMA, New Granada,
Lion's Den, OCT. 1, 1852.

TO GEN. PLATES, COL. T. CUPP, LT.-COL. SAUCER, *and* MAJ. POTT.

Gentlemen, — At a large and respectable meeting held by your guests this evening, in the bar room of your exquisite hotel.

A. Dodge, Esq., of Texas, was called to the Chair, and Kosciusko Blatherskite, of New Foundland, chosen Secretary.

On motion of Capt. Flatbroke, a committee was appointed to draft resolutions, expressive of the sense of the meeting, consisting of Mr. Dunep, Dr. Busted, and Capt. Flatbroke, who retired a few minutes, and returned with the following preamble and resolutions:

Whereas, it becomes us all to be grateful and benevolent to all who treat us with impunity; we cannot therefore resist the incumbent duty that is now forced to devolve upon us, of expressing at the following time our sentiments in regard to our kind reception, elegant entertainment and genteel treatment by Messrs. Plates & Co., the worthable proprietors of the Lion's Den, in this city; and when we think on the above, we would, in our unitarian capacity, give emitterance to the following resolutions:

Resolved 1st.— That since we landed at Aspinwall, we have been treated awfully by everybody, and plundered beside, except General Plates & Co.

Resolved 2nd.— That we advise hereby most earnestly all our friends, who intend to cross the Isthmus, to go by the way of Cape Horn.

Resolved 3rd.— That we deem the Lion's Den at Panama, under its present management, equal to any house in the United States, and rather a-head of the Astor House and Lovejoy's Hotel.

Resolved 4th.— That we consider General Plates & Co. perfect gentlemen, and that they spare no pains or expense to appear so.

Resolved 5th.— That we caution all travelers across this Isthmus against the Montebanks and the Peter Funks on this route, for our experience calls forth our most bitter indignation as American citizens.

Resolved 6th.— That the proceedings of this meeting be presented to General Plates & Co. and published in the Panama papers, the New York

Courier and Enquirer, Harper's Monthly Magazine, and the Farmers' Almanac, for 1853.

(Signed) A. Dodge, Chairman.
K. Blatherskite, Sec.
And 1600 others.

Gen. Plates.— (*Smiling.*) — Well, boys, this is doing the fair thing. Never mind the bills, they aint much any how, I reckon. Walk up and liquor. [All imbibe an infusion of pokeberries and alcohol, and exeunomnes, mutually delighted with each other.]

SQUIBOB.

X.

A TRIP TO OREGON.

On the 16th day of September I received a letter from my correspondent in Australia which convinced me that flour was about to make an unprecedented and unheard of rise. I have been nipped slightly heretofore in flour speculations; green and inviting appeared the floury paths before my mental vision, and I regret to say that I returned from their pursuit with just a shade of the greenness adhering to me, in a figurative point of view; but this time I determined to make a sure thing of it.

The last quotations from Oregon, (which land I never hear mentioned without associating it with the idea of Bartlett pears at one dollar a piece and particularly rotten inside) showed that flour might be purchased there for five dollars per barrel. "If, then," said I to Mrs. Butterfield, "I repair to Oregon, my dear, and purchase two thousand barrels of flour at five dollars per barrel, and re turning to San Francisco, incontinently sell the same at eleven dollars per ditto, our circumstances will be slightly improved."

Mrs. Butterfield had seen at Guerin's a perfect love of a velvet mantle; a brown velvet mantle profusely embroidered, for which they asked but one hundred and twenty-five dollars, and she said she thought "it would be a good thing." And so I went down to the steamship Columbia, and purchased "A" stateroom, and had my trunk "dragged into camp" in stateroom "A." I detest and despise going to sea; it makes me sick at my stomach and I cannot agree with that young man who, on being reminded that "a rolling stone gathers no moss," replied, "never mind the moss — *let us roll.*" I do not like to roll at all, and I sincerely believe that the man who first invented going to sea was some most abandoned rascal, who could not under any circumstances be permitted to live on shore, and I wish from my heart he had been drowned, and the invention lost with him. So that when I had paid sixty dollars to Purser

Meade, who like the beverage that bears his name, is of a mild though sparkling disposition, and is moreover constantly effervescing with good humor, I went below, and gazing with a discontented air at stateroom "A," thought to myself I had given a very high price for an emetic. However, when one has made up his mind to be slain, it is certainly the best plan to employ a regular physician and have it done *secundum artem*, and it was a great relief to my mind to find the Columbia a clean and comfortable steamship, where if one had to die, he could at least die with decency. The Captain too had such a cheery good natured smile on his handsome face, such a roguish twinkle about his eye, such a strong expression of wishing to make every one happy about him that it was difficult to conceive that anything very disagreeable could happen where he commanded.

You must have heard of the "Dalls of the Columbia." Well, that may appear a slight digression, but the Captain is "one of them." The Columbia went to sea and I went to bed in the second berth in stateroom "A." As Lever's hero,

Charles O'Malley, invariably, remarks, after getting a lick on the back of the head, "I knew nothing more" until the arrival at Mendocino Mills. Confused visions of Mrs. Butterfield, nursing a fifty lb. sack of flour, which changed occasionally into a bowl of gruel, and then into a large wash basin, prevailed in my mind, I remember, during this period; but at Mendocino Mills I arose, girded up my loins, and the Columbia being very quiet, came forth like a young giant refreshed with new wine. In fact, as the Captain pleasantly remarked, I "opened like a psalm book."

Even a tortoise draweth suddenly in his head when smote from the rear by some evil disposed urchin with a stick; so suddenly did I disappear within the shell of stateroom "A," when the Columbia left Mendocino Mills. Then an interval elapsed, and we arrived at Trinidad. This place derives its name from the Latin words *Trinis*, three, and *Dad*, father, having been originally discovered by three Catholic priests. The town consists of about thirty mules, being packed with whiskey for the mines on Trinity river. Another interval of wash basin and gruel and we anchored at Crescent City. This little place has quite an active and bustling appearance. It is the depot of the Klamath mines, and appears to be very much of a business place. At the door of the principal public house, sat a forlorn, lost looking girl, who had once been beautiful; she was neatly and handsomely dressed, but there was a look of suffering about her pale and care worn face that I shall not soon forget. I was told she was the proprietor of the establishment. Poor thing.

There is some surf at Crescent City, and unless you embark cautiously you are very liable to get your trowsers wet. I never do anything cautiously. We arrived at Port Oxford one night, and disembarked Lieut. Kautz and eight mules belonging to the 4th U. S. Infantry. Lieut. Kautz commands the military post at Port Oxford I was told, but what the military post is, I am not informed; probably they use it to tie the mules to. Port Oxford is a small place, a very small place! I heard that the Columbia once got up steam and left here, without casting off one of her stern lines, and accidentally towed the whole city up the coast about forty miles before the line parted, very much to the confusion of one Tichnor, who having been elected a member of the Oregon Legislature, sailed off in a small schooner to find that body, but being unsuccessful, attempted to return to Port Oxford but did not get in for some time owing to that accident.

Imagine the feelings that animated my mind as we arrived — I sprang hastily from the steamer; I saw my friend Mr. Leonard G. Green, the great Portland jobber and importer, on the dock. I seized him by the arm and led him one side — "Butterfield," said he, "how do you do?" "Never mind," replied I, in a faltering voice; "I want to buy two thousand barrels of Oregon flour!"

Leonard G. Green smiled; he was not at all excited, and he answered "Probably!"— I gasped for breath. "Tell me," said I "how is flour selling?" Leonard G. Greene looked me calmly in the eye and answered slowly "Eleven dollars and a half a barrel!" I am not a profane man; I attend the Rev. Dr. Scott's church regularly, have family prayers in my household, and say grace over my frugal repasts; but dog-gorn —— never mind, as the man said "I couldn't begin to do justice to the subject."

I wrote a letter, a doleful letter to Mrs. Butterfield that night, and the brown velvet embroidered mantle, still hangs in Austin's window.

I walked up the street of Portland and heard a man scream out, "J. Neely Johnston is Governor of California, ha! ha! ha!" Confound Portland and Oregon Teritory; I wish from the very bottom of my heart that Pierce would appoint John Bigler Governor of it.

Yours in deep disgust,

AMOS BUTTERFIELD.

Flour and Pork

Near the corner of Battery and Front

Orders from the country promptly filled.

XI.

BUTTERFIELD AT THE BALL.

You have not heard from me for some time. I have been "round," however, which is a pleasant metaphorical way of expressing the fact that I have been about, and is not intended as an allusion to my figure, though I weigh two hundred and forty-three net, and it might appear appropriate to scoffers. Since my unfortunate expedition to Oregon, I have been attending closely to my legitimate business, and do not mind saying that I have been tolerably successful. I did a little thing in butter last week, not after the manner of the celebrated sculptor Canova — who, I am told, used to carve horses and other animals out of that oleaginous substance, which looked well but became unpleasant to the smell in a short time — but in the way of speculation, which increased my satisfaction and my balance at Doolittle, Walker & Leggett's, my bankers, in no small degree.

I was sitting in my counting-room a few days since, in an amiable frame of mind, thinking of that butter which I had sold to a manufacturer to grease the wheels of his manufactory, and wondering whether its strength increased the power of the machinery, when Podgers, of Gawk & Podgers, Battery street, dropped in. "Butterfield," said he, "don't you want to go to a ball?" A vision of Mrs. Butterfield resplendent in her new dress, which, though of late importation, she calls "*more antique*," passed before my mind. I thought of the balance at Doolittle's, and in my usual prompt and decided manner replied, "Well, I don't know." "It's a complimentary ball," said Podgers, given for the benefit of the officers of the Army and Navy, and comes off at Madame Pike's on Friday. (The name is Pique, and is pronounced *Pi-quee*, but Podgers don't understand French." Now I always liked the officers, poor fellows; they look so prettily in their brass-mounted clothes, and walk around with such a melancholy air, as though they were wondering how they manage to support existence on their pay and allowance — and how the deuce they do puzzles me. So after a few words more with Podgers, we started off to purchase the necessary pasteboard. I suppose it was because the ball was a national affair that we went to the United States Mint for that purpose. Here we were introduced to a singularly handsome young fellow, who gazed rather dubiously on Podgers and myself when he preferred our request. "The ball is to be very select," said he. "Ah," replied I, "that's exactly the reason we wish to patronize it." The young gentleman could not withstand the smile with which these words were accompanied. "What name?" said he. "Butterfield," I replied. "Flour and Pork," said he, with a kindly expression. "Corner of Battery and Front," I answered, and the thing was done. Podgers got his ticket also, and we left the Mint arm in arm, wondering if the lovely design for a head on the new three dollar piece was intended for a likeness of the U. S. Treasurer, of whose agreeable countenance we caught a glimpse as we retired. Mrs. Butterfield was delighted, so was Austin, I fancy; he sent me a note a day or two after, very prettily conceived, with Honiton, Valenciennes, point, edging, and other hard words in it, which must have given him great satisfaction to compose. I purchased of Keyes (not that Keyes, but the other firm) a new blue dress coat with brazen buttons, military, you know; a pair of cinnamon colored leg scabbards, and a very tasty thing in the way of a vest, garnet colored velvet with green plush cross bars, in which I fancied I should create something of a sensation. I also dropped in at Tucker's, and seeing a pretty breastpin in the form of a figure 2, which he said was a tasteful conceit for married men, showing that there were two in the family, I bought that also, and hereby acknowledge that it has given me great satisfaction. Friday evening at last arrived. Podgers was to come for us in a carriage at 8 o'clock, and we commenced dressing at three, immediately after dinner. My friends have sometimes flattered me by remarking something in my air and personal appearance resembling the late eloquent Daniel Webster (formerly Secretary of State under Tyler's administration.) After dressing, and going through the operation which Mrs. Butterfield unpleasantly terms prinking, I walked into the room of our next neighbor, (we board at the corner of Stockton and Powell) under the pretence of borrowing a candle. He was sitting by the fire smoking a cigar and reading Tennyson's poems, which I take this opportunity of declaring are the silliest trash I ever had the misfortune to get hold of.

"Mr. Brummell," said I complacently, "do you think I look at all like the great Daniel?" Brumell gazed on me with evident admiration. "Yes," he replied, "but you are not near as heavy as he was." "No?" said I, "Why, Daniel Webster was not a *very* large man." "Oh!" replied he,

"I thought you alluded to Daniel Lambert." This was a damper.

We worked for three mortal hours getting little Amos to sleep. That child is two years of age, possesses a wakefulness of disposition perfectly astonishing in one so young, and has a pleasing peculiarity of howling terrifically in the night at intervals of about twenty-five minutes. Paregoric and taffy were too much for him this time, however; he succumbed at last, and dropped peacefully to repose at half-past seven, to a second. At eight, Podgers and the carriage arrived. Mrs. Podgers came up in Mrs. Butterfield's room to show herself. She was tastefully and magnificently attired. She wore a white crape illusion with eighteen flounces, over a profusely embroidered tulle skirt, looped up on the side with a bouquet of Swiss meringues. Her boddice was of sea-green tabbinet, with an elegant pincushion of orange-colored *moire antique* over the bertha. Her head-dress was composed of cut velvet cabbage leaves, with turnip *au naturel*, and a small boned turkey secured by a golden wire, "*a la maitre d' hotel*," crowned the structure. Podgers gazed upon her with complacent and pardonable pride. We descended to the carriage, but finding it impossible for all of us to ride within, Mrs. Podgers stood upon the seat with the driver, Mrs. Butterfield and I got inside, and Podgers walked. [By the way, on this account, he subsequently, in an unjustifiable manner, objected to paying his proportion of the expenses of transportation, as had been agreed upon between us.] On arriving at Mrs. Pique's, I regret to say, an unpleasant altercation took place between myself and our driver on the subject of the fare. I was finally compelled to close the discussion by disbursing ten dollars, which that disagreeable individual unnecessarily remarked, "was only a dollar a hundred after all." On entering the hall, which was brilliantly illuminated, we were struck with its size and elaborate ornaments, and also with the unpleasant fact that nobody was there. The fact is, we had arrived a little too early. However, we amused ourselves walking about, and Podgers got into the supper room, where he broke a sugar chicken off the top of a large cake, to carry home to his little Anna Maria, and being detected therein, was summarily ejected, and had the chicken taken away from him, at which Mrs. B. and I secretly rejoiced. At ten o'clock, the company began to arrive, and in half an hour the large hall was crowded with the beauty, fashion and extravagance of the city. It really brought tears of delight to my eyes to see the number of lovely women that San Francisco can produce, and to think what immense sums of money their beautiful dresses must cost their husbands and fathers. Sets of quadrilles were formed, then followed the fancy dances, polkas, redowas, and that funny dance where the gentleman grabs the lady about the waist with one hand, and pumps her arm up and down with the other, while hopping violently from side to side, after the manner of that early and estimable Christian — St. Vitus. I cannot pretend to enumerate the ladies whose charms particularly impressed me. Moreover, if

I could, it would be of little service to the public, for it is in the fashion to do this sort of thing by initials, and who would recognize "lovely Mrs. A., with her ugly daughter, in white cottonet, and magnificent Mrs. B., the cynosure of all eyes in a *peignoir* of three ply carpeting, with a *corsage de gunny bag* and a *point appliqué robe de nuit*, or the sweet Misses C. in elaborate Swiss ginghams, with gimp cord and tassels and a *fauteuil de cabriolet.* Suffice it to say that the loveliest ladies of San Francisco were there, and the belle of the evening was unquestionably Miss ——, though many preferred the mature charms of the radiant Mrs. ——. [You perceive that these blanks are left for the convenience of those who wish to send this description to the Eastern States, who hereby have my express permission to insert any names they may think appropriate.] One lady, I observed, whose dress, though no great judge of dry goods, I should imagine to have cost in the neighborhood of fifty barrels of mess pork. Everything went off admirably. Wobbles, of Wobbles &

Strycum, who was present with his daughter, a young lady of nine years, with a violent propensity to long curls, dressed in crimson silk with orange colored pantalettes. Wobbles, who has a very pretty way of saying poetical things, remarked with great originality, that "soft eyes spoke love to eyes that spoke again, and all went berry as a marriage mell," and I agreed with him.

The officers were all there, moreover, radiant in brass coats and blue buttons — I mean blue buttons and brass coats — and looking divinely. One of them accidently trod on my toe, but before I could utter the exclamation of anguish that I was about to give vent to, he said so sweetly "Don't apologise," that the pain left me in a moment. "The officers of the Vincennes, though sufficiently handsome are not tall men. This, Podgers remarked, was a dispensaton of Divine Providence, as the Vincennes is only four feet six between decks, and they would be constantly bumping their heads if they were taller.

At two o'clock we sat down to supper. Magnificent indeed — turkeys, chickens, salads, champagne — everybody gobbling and guzzling everything, presenting to my mind a far finer spectacle than the vaunted Falls of Niagara, which I think have been much overrated.

Podgers, who is always doing something unpleasant, emptied a plate of oyster soup on my head, merely saying, "Beg pardon, Butterfield," in consequence of which I found a large stewed oyster in my right whisker on returning to the ball room, and was made exceedingly uncomfortable during the rest of the morning.

The ball was delightful. I heard the Consul of New Zealand say it was *ravissant*, and though with but a dim idea of his meaning, I am sure it was. We returned home at 3 ½ A. M. The street around our residence was lighted up as if for a celebration; people stood around the door-steps, and an old gentleman with a watchman's rattle in his hand, both slightly sprung, was leaning out of an upper window of No. 3 below. A loud shout hailed us as we approached, but high above that shout, loud above the whirr of the rattle, shrill above the rolling of our carriage, sounded an alarum that we recognized but too well. It was the voice of our little Amos. The dear child had woke up the whole street, and it is a marvel that he had not awakened the sleepers in John Jones of Peter's cemetery, "just beyond." For — the name of Butterfield, as you well know, is synonymous with that of Truth, — but if that boy hadn't shattered every pane of glass in our front windows, and loosened all the top bricks of the chimney by the concussion of the air produced by his screaming, I wish I may never sell another lot of extra clear bacon. The paper was loosened from the walls, the plaster falling from the ceiling, the wash basin and ——, everything was broken, and there lay Amos black in the face, gurgling in his throat, and his small blue legs kicking up toward Heaven. We did not get asleep until rather late that morning, and what with damages, repairs, hack, drivers, dresses and tickets, the little balance at Doolittle, Walker & Leggett's is nearly exhausted.

Perhaps we shall go to another ball at Madame Pique's, soon, if so, I will send you an account of it.

Very truly yours,

AMOS BUTTERFIELD,

Flour and Pork,

Corner of Battery and Front streets.

Country orders solicited and promptly filled, etc.

DARK INFANTRY—AN ASS-SAULT.—*See page* 125.

XII.

SQUIBOB'S "COMPOSITION OF ARMIES,"

A NEW METHOD OF ATTACK AND DEFENCE OF POSTS.

The subject of composition of Armies, that of fortification, and the attack and defense of military posts, have for many years been considered of the first importance to the safety and welfare of nations, and have in consequence, been elaborately treated of by Vauban, Cormontaigne and other eminent scientific men, of their own and later periods.

With the advance of civilization, refinement and scientific discovery, we should naturally be led to expect new discoveries and improvements in these important branches of the military art.

Such is however by no means the case. Whether a state of peace has operated unfavorably to the prosecution of military research, or that the great minds of modern philosophers are turned exclusively to such sources of discovery as may operate more to their personal emolument than to the benefit of future generations, it is useless to discuss, — true it is, however, that in all essential particulars the art of war remains in precisely the same state that it was left by the savans who wrote upon it half a century ago.

Feeling deeply the necessity of some more perfect means of defence than these comparatively uneducated and uninformed writers have left us, the writer remembering the maxim of the immortal Washington, "In time of peace prepare for war," has devoted himself exclusively for two days to the most close and vigorous research into the principles of the military art, and has finally, by combining the most valuable ideas of the more scientific writers slightly modified by some originality of his own, obtained a system of defence which he thinks more suited to the present advanced stage of science.

This system he would present with becoming

deference and humility to the approval of his brother officers, with the hope that they will think it peculiarly adapted to the defence of our own beloved country, when left, in accordance with the message of a late executive, to the tender mercies of armed steamboats and the militia.

And first, with regard to the composition of armies for offensive operations in the field. For this purpose let a body of men between the ages of eighteen and forty-five be selected, if for immediate active service, blacks should be selected, as being undoubtedly more *offensive* than whites. These men, after being properly drilled to act in concert, should be armed in the following manner. Each man to be provided with one of Colt's patent revolving six-barreled rifles, with the necessary ammunition.

2d. A large tin case perforated with holes on the top, is to be filled with black pepper and suspended by the right side.

3d. A dress cap made of tin and lined with flannel, the top of which is a cylinder containing the material for generating sulphuretted hydrogen gas, with a stop-cock in front, opening by the pressure of a spring, immediately over his right ear. Each man on being enlisted should be furnished with a staunch and well trained bull-dog, which he will take the greatest possible care of, and which he should teach carefully to come and go at his command. (*See Page* 128.)

Both men and dogs should be accustomed by frequent drills to the odor of the gas they carry about them, and should be exercised frequently with their pepper pots before being taken into the field. Sneezing on such occasions should be looked upon as a serious military delinquency, and treated accordingly. These preliminary steps being taken, the troops are ready for service.

On the eve of a battle, they will throw up a continuous line in their front, consisting of a parapet and ditch of the usual form and dimensions.

On the advance of the enemy they open a rapid and severe fire with their revolving rifles, which must of course appal and disconcert the enemy.

On the slightest symptoms of retreat, the bull-dogs will be loosed and encouraged to charge the retreating foe. This they will do en masse, and seizing the unhappy wretches by the seats of their trowsers, will delay their progress or drag them back within close rifle shot. This will generally decide the affair. If, however, in consequence of vast numbers or determined bravery, the enemy advance to the trench, a warm fire must be kept up.

On coming to close quarters, tne men will use their pepper pots vigorously. Nothing can withstand this system, — with eyes smarting and blinded with pepper, noses offended with the stench of the parapet, deafened by the barking of the dogs and incessantly annoyed by their sharp and tenacious gripe, the enemy, though composed of the best materials that ever made up an army, must give way and fall an easy prey in their torturing retreat, to our victorious arms.

When flying artillery is used in connection with

these troops, it will consist of four and six pound field-pieces, carefully strapped on the backs of stout jackasses and pointed to the rear. These being fired the recoil will arouse all the natural obstinacy of the animal, who, thinking he is pushed forward, will instantly move stern first, with incredible celerity, towards the enemy. When a retreat is ordered, the men serving the gun will pull the beast's tail, who will immediately change his motion and rush forward with impetuosity. It is thus that man shows his supremacy over the brute creation, in rendering even their evil dispositions subservient to his designs. (*See Page* 128.)

The next subject proposed for our consideration, is that of fortification.

We have seen in the works of Vauban, Mahan, Cormontaigne etc., that in following their various systems, — however well we may fortify a place, however carefully we may defilade our works, and satisfy the conditions imposed as requisite to a good defence, we are still unable to render a place impregnable. It is acknowledged by all writers upon this subject, that the beseigers have an advantage over the beseiged, which however well it may be defended, will inevitably lead sooner or later to the capture of their work. With this great principle established, our course is a very simple one. In fortifying a particular site, let the space to be occupied by the garrison be entirely inclosed by a continuous line of bastioned fronts, constructed according to the most approved modern system.

There will however, be this slight difference, — all the salients will be directed inwards, toward the common centre, and the gorges of the bastions, demi-lunes, etc., turned outward, and left entirely unprotected. This will give the garrison all the advantages claimed by the besiegers; for the besieging army marching up, will immediately occupy the works from without. The garrison having, in expectation of this movement, made the necessary preparations, will instantly commence the construction of parallels, boyaux, etc., and in forty nights with the assistance of divine providence, and in accordance with our distinguished authority, infallibly carry the place, thus completely turning the tables on their adversaries.

In constructing the trenches, the mens' coats should be carefully lined behind with sheet-iron, and thus rendered musket proof. This will prevent the necessity of defiling the trenches from a severe fire, — if indeed the bull-dogs have not already defiled them sufficiently.

The writer will here leave the subject. It is however his intention to submit these notes to the War department, and if his sanguine expectations should be realized, his system adopted, and he should meet with that reward which he modestly believes his suggestions deserve, — an immediate brevet, — he assures his comrades that he shall never consider himself in the least elevated above them. He will always be happy to meet them, and if they should be so fortunate as to receive commissions in regiments formed upon his system, he can recommend them a man who will sell them most excellent bull-dogs of a fierce and savage breed, — and pepper-pots of a new and peculiar construction.

XIII.

BOSTON — A MORAL CITY.

It is Sunday in Boston. I have been sitting in my room, No. 78 Tremont House; by the window, which commands a cheerful view of a graveyard, musing on various matters and things in a solemn state of mind well befitting the place and the occasion. Seventeen inches of snow fell last night, and Boston looks white like the Island of Ichaboe, and to the full as desolate. Through the hollow and reverberating passages of this ancient building; around the corners of the sinuous streets; from each door and window, in every private and public building, and from the houses of God, resounds the peculiar sharp, hacking cough of the population of Boston. Every soul of them has it. It is the disease of the country. When I meet an acquaintance in the street, I abstain from the usual greeting, and invariably say, "How is your cough?" and the reply invariably is, "About the same." Coughing, and the ancient pastime of hawking, (followed by expectoration,) are the principal amusements in this cold city. In the grave-yard beneath my window, on a slate tombstone, may be found, I am informed, the following touching inscription:

"Here I lie bereft of breath,
Because a cough carried me off,
Then a coffin, they carried me off in;"

which, I doubt not, describes the case of the majority of the silent incumbents of that place of rest.

The Tremont House is in many respects a good institution; it is perfectly clean and well arranged, the attendance is good and the fodder excellent; but there is an indescribable air of gloom and solemnity pervades the entire establishment well suited to Boston, but chilling to a stranger to the last degree. The waiters, dressed in black with white neckcloths, move silently and sadly about the tables, looking like so many Methodist ministers with thirteen children, four hundred a year, and two donation parties; the man in the office never smiles — in any point of view; a large Bible with the name of the House stamped upon it in gilt letters, (to prevent religious strangers from bottling it,) lies on every table, and the chambermaids attend family prayers in the basement. All is "grand, gloomy," and it must be confessed, exceedingly peculiar. I have attempted but two jokes in this solemn place, and they fell like the flakes of snow, silent and unnoticed. An unfortunate individual in the reading-room last evening was seized with an unusually violent fit of coughing, which, if a man could by any possibility be turned inside out, would have done it; and as a partial cessation of it occurred, with his hair standing on end, (he had coughed his hat off,) his face glowing with exertion, and the tears standing in his unhappy eyes, he very naturally gave vent to a profane execration. Every body looked shocked! I remarked in an audible tone to my companion, that the exclamation was a coffer-dam; an admirable contrivance for raising obstructions from the bottom of streams, and probably adopted by the gentleman to clear his throat; but no one laughed, and I incontinently went to bed.

This morning on arising I discovered that my boots, left outside the door to be embellished with blacking, had, like those of Bombastes, not been displaced; so I said to the porter, a man of grave and solemn aspect: "You have a very honest set of people about this house." "Why?" said the porter, with a somewhat startled expression. "Because," I rejoined, "I left my boots outside my door last night, and find this morning no one has touched them." That man walked off all slow and stately, and never knew that I had been humorous.

Disappointments have been my lot in life. I remember in early childhood going to the theatre to see Mrs. W. H. Smith appear in two pieces; the bills said she would do it, and she came on the stage perfectly whole and entire like any other lady. Upon the whole it is my impression that Boston is a dull, gloomy, precise, and solemn city, which I take to be owing entirely to the intense cold that prevails there in the winter, which chills and freezes up the warmer nature of the inhabitants, who don't have time to get thawed out before the cold comes back again. I have met many Bostonians in more genial climates, who appeared to be very hearty and agreeable fellows.

I took a short ride yesterday in the Metropolitan Rail-Road cars, which are dragged by horse-power from the Tremont House to Roxbury. The only other occupant of my car was a young and lovely female in deep mourning. She wore a heavy, black veil, and her thick and auburn hair was gathered up on each side her face beneath a spotless cap, a widow's cap of snowy muslin. I had always a feeling for widows; young and pretty widows particularly, always excite my deepest interest and sympathy. I gazed with moistened eye on the sweet specimen before me, so young, so beautiful, I thought, and alas! what suffering she has experienced. I pictured to myself her devotion to her husband during his last illness, the untiring watchfulness with which she hung over his pillow, the unwearying and self-sacrificing spirit with which she hoped on, hoped ever, till in despite of her care, her love, he sank forever, and her agonized shriek rang in my ear, as with hands clasped and upturned eye, she felt that he was dead, her dream of life was over, her strength was gone, her heart was broken. The young widow had been regarding me earnestly during this time, and probably imagined what was passing in my mind, for throwing her veil over her hat, she turned partly around toward me, and looking steadfastly in my face — she winked her eye! Yes, sir, she winked her eye at *me* — the moral Phœnix; and I rose from my ashes and left the metropolitan car and returned to the Tremont House.

They don't have theatrical performances in Boston on Saturday evenings; the theaters open at 3 o'clock P. M., and the performance is over at six. Thalberg was allowed to give a concert here last evening, however. He was practising a little this morning also on the piano, when a message came from a serious family in the next room begging him not to play dancing tunes. He didn't.

I had intended to have written to you more at length, but am off to New Orleans directly, and must pack my trunk. Boston is a great place. I am sorry I hadn't time to go and see the Monastery presided over by Abbot Lawrence, that was burned by the Orangemen.

Yours truly and respectfully,

JOHN PHŒNIX.

XIV.

A JOURNEY FROM BOSTON TO NEW ORLEANS.

New Orleans, La. 1857.

On the fifth of January, at eight A. M., I left the Tremont House in a hackney carriage, the wheels whereof had turned into runners. This method of progression, rendered necessary by the deep snows, is considered a great amusement in the North. Being particularly dangerous to life and limb, and usually terminating in pulmonary consumption, the pastime is very properly called sleighing.

With a through-ticket for the great city of Cairo in my pocket, I took a seat in the cars at the Worcester rail-road depot. After waiting half-an-hour, during which time my sympathies were deeply interested by the performance of an unhappy young couple, one of whom was going somewhere and the other wasn't, and who in consequence were slobbering over each other to a terrible extent, a sudden harsh bark was heard from the engine, a grating jar, which acted on my teeth like lemon-juice, followed, and we were off. The motion of a rail-road car is of two kinds, which may be called the "heave and set, or whip-saw movement," and the "tip and sifter," names sufficiently expressive to require no farther explanation. We started on the "heave and set," which gradually merged into the "tip and sifter" as our velocity increased.

On entering a rail-road car the first object of the solitary traveller should be to secure an entire seat to himself. This may generally be done successfully by taking the outside seat and skilfully disposing a small carpet-bag, great coat, umbrella, and cane, so as to cover the inner one. As the passengers throng into the car, many will gaze earnestly at the place thus occupied, but will usually prefer to move on rather than give you trouble; but if the car is quite filled, the question will undoubtedly be asked, "Is that seat taken,

Sir?" when you should reply with an imperturbable countenance, "It is, Sir! and the inquirer, with perhaps a slight glance of suspicion, will move on. As a man's object should be to make himself as comfortable as possible in this world, that his mind may be in a proper frame to prepare for the next, a slight deviation from truth for the purpose of securing this object, like the above, is quite pardonable, in which opinion I am corroborated by my dear friend and Christian teacher, Rev. H. B. — tch — s, whose celebrated and useful aphorism, "Never lie, unless it is necessary," will doubtless recur to the reader's mind.

Having made my arrangements in accordance with these views, and being as comfortable as circumstances would permit, the motion of the cars being that of a small boat in a high sea, and their noise like unto a steam saw-mill, I composed myself to the journey. At Framingham the usual nuisances of rail-road cars commenced. First appeared the small boy with the Boston newspapers, which had been brought to him by our train ; then the dirty boy, with the parched corn, who, in the intervals of trade, dabbles among his merchandise with his sore hand, and devours so much of that dry commodity, that you are fain to believe him to be his own best customer ; then the big boy, with the fearful apples, " three for five cents ;" and finally that well-known, and most indefatigable wretch with the " lozengers," who on this occasion actually sold a roll of the description called " checkerberry " to an elderly individual of the Muggins family sitting near me, who eat them, and to my great joy, became wofully disordered in consequence. But the boy with the accordeon was not there — I think he has not yet got so far North. It was but a week before that I met him, however on the Philadelphia cars. It was after eleven o'clock ; the train had passed New Brunswick, and the passengers were trying to sleep, (ha ! ha !) when the boy entered. He was a seedy youth, with a seal-skin cap, a singularly dirty face, a gray jacket of the ventilating order, and a short but remarkably broad pair of "corduroy-corduroys." He wore an enormous bag or haversack about his neck, and bore in his hand that most infernal and detestable instrument, an accordeon. I despise that instrument of music. They pull the music out of it, and it comes forth struggling and reluctant, like a cat drawn by the tail from an ash-hole or a squirrel pulled shrieking from a hollow log with a ram-rod. This unprincipled boy commenced pulling at his thing and horrified us with the most awful version of that wretched "Dog Tray" that I ever listened to. Then he walked around the car and collected forty-two cents. Then he returned to the center of the car, and standing close to the stove, which was red hot — the night being cold — he essayed to pull out "Pop Goes the Weasel," when suddenly pop went the boy; he dropped the accordeon, burst into tears, and clapping his hands behind him, executed a frantic dance, accompanied by yells of the most agonizing character. I saw it all, and felt grateful to a retributive Providence. He had stood too close to the stove and his corduroys were in a light blaze; a few inches below the termination of the gray jacket was the seat of his wo. After he got on fire the conductor put him out, and a sweet and ineffable calm came over me. I realized that "whatever is, is right," and I fell into a deep and happy sleep.

The musical nuisance, fortunately was spared us on this occasion. A tourist travelling by railroad across the United States would have but little opportunity to collect notes for his forthcoming work. Thus my idea of Albany, at which Dutch village we arrived shortly after dark, are, a hasty scramble down a platform; then huddling into a sled with other bewildered and half-frozen passengers; then a rapid foot-race of about a quarter of a mile, encouraged by shouts of "Leg it! the cars are off." "No they aint; plenty of time." "Hi! hi! there, round the corner, them's the cars," etc.; then more cars and we ground on.

It was on this Albany and Buffalo train that a little incident occurred which may be worthy of mention, and serve as a caution to future innocent travellers. I had observed that at each change of cars, and they were frequent, when the general scramble took place, one car was defended from the assault by a stalwart man, usually of the Irish persuasion, who deaf to menaces, unsoftened by entreaty, and uncorrupted by bribes, maintained his post for the benefit of the "leddies." "Leddies car, Sir, av ye please; forrid cars for gintlemen without leddies." Need I say that this car so reserved was by the far most comfortable of the train, and that with that stern resolve which ever distinguishes me in the discharge of my duty toward myself, I determined to get into it *coute qui coute*. So when we changed cars at Utica, I rushed forth, and seeing a nice young person, with a pretty face, bonnet and shawl, and a large portmanteau, urging her way through the crowd, I stepped up by her side and with my native grace and gallantry offered my arm and my assistance. They were gratefully accepted, and proud of my success, I ushered my fair charge up to the platform of the ladies' car. My old enemy was holding the door. "Is that your lady, Sir?" said he. With an inward apology to Mrs. Phœnix for the great injustice done to her charms by the admission, I replied: "Yes." Judge of my horror when this low employée of a monopolizing and unaccommodating rail-road company addressing my companion with the tone and manner of an old acquaintance, said: "Well, Sal, I guess you've done well, but I don't believe his family will think much of the match." However, I got into the ladies' car and having repudiated the young person Sarah, got an exceedingly pleasant seat by the side of a very warm and comfortable young lady of a sleepy turn and quiet disposition. I wouldn't have exchanged her for two buffalo-robes, but alas! she got off at Syracuse, and then, frosty Caucasus, how cold it was! And so grinding, and jolting, jarring, sliding, and freezing, wore away the long night.

In the morning we were at Buffalo. I saw nothing of it but a rail-road depot; but I remember thinking as I stamped my feet and thrashed my arms to restore the circulation, that if that sort of weather continued, "the Buffalo girls couldn't come out to-night," and would probably have to postpone their appearance until the summer season.

Among the passengers on the Erie rail-road was a very interesting family, on their way to Terre Haute. (Ind.) There was the father, a fine manly figure; the mother, pale, delicate, and lady-like; and niece, cousins, and babies innumerable, but all pretty and pleasant to behold. But the gem of the family was "Belle." Belle was the factotum, she nursed the babies, went errands for her father, helped her mother, and was always on hand to render assistance to any body, anywhere; and though her patience must have been sorely tried, she preserved her amiability and genuine good nature so thoroughly that she became to me an object of constant attention and admiration. She was evidently the manager of that family, and went about every thing with a business-like air, quite refreshing to observe. She was about sixteen years old, very pretty, neatly dressed, and of a most merry and vivacious disposition, as was evinced by every sparkle of her bright eyes. Farewell, "Belle," probably you'll never see this tribute from your unknown admirer, or meet him in *propria personæ;* but the loss will hardly be felt, for you must have more admirers already than you know what to do with. Happy is the man that's destined to ring the Belle of Terre Haute.

All day and all night we ground on, "ripping and staving." We passed through Columbus where the people had been having a grand ball to celebrate the completion of their State Capitol, and picked up three hundred and eighty-four survivors, each of whom contained a pint and a half of undiluted whiskey. And so in the morning we came to Cincinnati, where for fifteen minutes we tarried at the Burnett House, the most magnificent hotel in these United States. Here I met with Fisher, the celebrated rail-road traveller, who accompanied us to Sandoval, and with whom I was particularly charmed. Fisher is the original inventor of that ingenious plan of getting rid of an unpleasant occupant of the same seat, by opening the window on the coldest night, so that the draught shall visit searchingly the back of the victim's neck; and of that method of taking up the seat and disposing it as an inclined plane, and going to sleep thereon in such a complicated manner as to defy subsequent intrusion. What he does not know about rail-roads is of no manner of consequence and useless to acquire. Thanks to his experience, we enjoyed the luxury of two seats together, and it was with deep regret that I parted with him at Sandoval. The change of cars from the Erie to the Illinois Central, is a delightful incident. The latter has the broad gauge, the seats are comfortable and convenient, the speed exhilarating, and no exertion is spared by the civil conductors to render the passengers as happy as circumstances will permit. I have never travelled more comfortably than on the Illinois Central, and hereby wish long life and prosperity to the company.

The third day and the third night were over, we had passed safely through the city of Sandoval, which consists of one house, where the cars are detained five hours for the benefit of an aged villain who gave us very poor roasted buzzard and called it wild turkey; and, grateful to Providence, we arrived at Grand Cairo.

I stepped out of the cars a shorter man than when I started. The friction for three days and three nights had reduced my height two-and-a-half inches; a singular psychological fact, which I recommend to the consideration of the learned Walker.

Cairo is a small hole at the junction of the Ohio and Mississippi River, surrounded by an artificial bank to prevent inundation. There are here about thirteen inhabitants, but the population is estimated at three thousand, that being a rough estimate of the number of people that were once congregated there, when five trains of cars arrived before a boat left for New Orleans. They were enjoying the luxury of the small-pox at Cairo when we arrived; they are always up to something of the kind; a continued succession of amusements follow. The small-pox having terminated its engagement, the cholera makes its appearance, and is then followed by yellow fever for the season. Sweet spot! Dickens has immortalized it under the name of Eden, an evident misnomer, for no man worth as much as Adam could remain there by any possibility.

The fine steamer "James Montgomery" was about to leave for New Orleans, and we soon found ourselves most comfortably, indeed luxuriously established on board. A very merry passage we had to this great Crescent City, under the charge of our stout and jovial captain, whose efforts to amuse us, seconded as he was by the pretty and vivacious "widow," were entirely successful. The "General" also, a noble specimen of the gentlemen of Tennessee, proved himself a most agreeable travelling companion, and endeared himself to our little society by his urbanity, cheerfulness and fund of amusing and interesting anec dotes. Among our passengers was, moreover, the celebrated Eliza Logan, probably the finest actress now on the American stage, who has acquired a most enviable popularity, not only by her great profesional talent, but by her charms of conversation and her estimable reputation as a lady. She chants the "Marseillaise" in a style that would delight its author. One who wishes to realize for an instant what death is, should listen to her enunciation of the last words of the refrain of this celebrated composition; if he can repress a shudder, he is something more or less than man. Accompanied by my old friend Butterfield, who had joined us at Memphis, I landed at New-Orleans, and proceeded forthwith to the Saint Charles Hotel. At this great tavern Amos expected to meet his wife, who had arrived from California, to rejoin him after a three months' separation. I never have seen a man so nervous. He rode on the outside of the coach with the driver, that he might obtain the earliest view of the building that contained his adored one. It was with great difficulty that I kept pace with him as he "tumultuously rushed" up the step leading to the Rotunda. In an instant he was at the office and gasping "Mrs. Butterfield." "In the parlor, Sir," replied Dan, and he was off. I followed and saw him stop with surprise as he came to the door. In the centre of the parlor stood Mrs. Butterfield. That admirable woman had adopted the very latest and most voluminous style; and having on a rich silk of greenish hue, looked like a lovely bust on the summit of a new-mown hay-stack. Butterfield was appalled for a moment, but hearing her cry "Amos," he answered hysterically, "My Amander!" and rushed on. He ran three times round Mrs. Butterfield, but it was of no use, he couldn't get in. He tried to climb her, but the hoops gave way and frustrated the attempt. He extended his arms to her; she held out hers to him; tears were in their eyes.

It was the most affecting thing I ever witnessed. Finally Mrs. Butterfield sat down, and Amos got behind the chair and kissed her, until their offspring, by howling and biting the calf of his leg, created a diversion. They were very happy, so were the people in the parlor. Every body appeared delighted; and a small boy, a year or two older than little Amos, jumped up and down like a whip-saw, and halloa'd "Hoop-ee" with all his might.

"Butterfield," said I, an hour or two later, "I suspect that Mrs. Butterfield has adopted hoops."

"Oh! yes," answered he, "I saw that sticking out. Perhaps it will obviate the little tendency she had to blow up. I'm glad of it."

I have taken room No. 3683 in this establishment, and am a looker on in Vienna. To be sure my view is that usually termed, "the bird's eye," but I am getting a tolerably good idea of things. I should like very much to attend the ordination of Brother Buchanan in March next, and hear the Russian Minister preach, but I fear it will be impossible.

You will hear from me when you receive my next letter. Respectfully yours.

JOHN PHŒNIX.

XV.

NEW ORLEANS — ITS HOTEL.

The St. Charles Hotel is a lively and bustling village of about one thousand inhabitants, pleasantly situated on the left bank of St. Charles street, which meanders through the centre of that sweet and swampy city, New Orleans.

The building presents a fine architectural appearance, being built of white lime-stone, and having in front a colonnade of massive pillars, which have a very imposing effect, in more than one sense, as they look like marble, and are in fact brick covered with stucco. But in spite of its conglomerate character, the structure is a fine one to gaze upon; and its inhabitants, owners, and New Orleans at large, are proud and happy in its possession, and well they may be. The "St. Charles" is the Mecca of the Southern States.

When the last bale of cotton has been shipped from the plantation and the last hogshead of sugar has followed it; when falling leaves and frosty mornings betoken the approach of winter; when the Spanish moss waves grandly from the lofty trees, alone in its verdure, and greasy niggers loll idly on the river banks, their large mouths watering over visions of "possum and hominy," then does the planter, rejoicing over the account of sales received from his agent, pack his trunks, gather together his family and prepare for his yearly pilgrimage. Having seen his family safely and comfortably bestowed in their luxurious state-rooms on board the floating palace that is to take him to New Orleans, he then proceeds to the "social hall," where, after indulging in sundry potent libations of corn-juice with a good set of fellows with whom he finds himself at once acquainted, our planter gladly accepts the invitation of an innocent-looking youth to play a little game of "euchre," "just for amusement." The game accordingly commences and the party are soon deeply engaged in the mysteries of "passing," "ordering up," and "going it alone." But the best of games becomes tiresome at last, and the planter feels relieved when one of the party proposes to change the game to "draw-poker" with a dime "ante," "just to make it interesting." Pokers are drawn and the battle has begun in serious earnest. Our planter has various success; now he is ten, perhaps twenty ahead, now five or ten "out," when suddenly, the innocent youth having the deal, he receives a hand of blissful promise, three queens, a seven, and four. How jealously our friend examines his hand, holding his cards tightly together and moving them just sufficiently to be quite sure there is no mistake about it. Then with a careless laugh he discards the worthless seven and four, and says he believes he'll "go in." They all "go in," and a mass of silver, with one or two aged and crumpled shin-plasters, adorns the centre of the table. The innocent youth deals, and our planter, to his great satisfaction, receives a pair of nines. He slips his cards hastily together, lays them on the table and awaits the result of the betting. The red-nosed man on his right "goes a five;" the man with the battered hat opposite, sees that and goes ten better; the innocent youth "passes," and our planter, in a voice tremulous with emotion, "sees" the last bet and "goes fifty better." The man with the red nose groans and asks if he may take down his money, but the man with the battered hat, pushing that article of dress still farther down over his sinister brow, puts his hands in his pocket and pulls forth the money. Here it is, twenty, forty, sixty, "two hundred dollars better!" The planter is surprised. He takes another secret but earnest glance at his cards. "A full," it can't be beaten. Out comes the old pocket-book, and he "calls." "*Four kings*," says the man with the battered hat, and with the most business-like air imaginable rakes down the money with one hand and turns over his cards with the other.

Our planter is disgusted, he leaves the table with an imprecation referring to the soul of the innocent youth, takes more corn juice, and excepting a little dash at "chuck-a-luck" at which he loses seven dollars and wins a horn-handled knife and a pocket-book, tempts fortune no farther during the voyage. Meanwhile the innocent youth and his comrades divide the money in the "barber's shop," and go on shore at the next landing, well pleased with their success.

On arriving at the St. Charles the planter's party are supplied with a parlor and the necessary sleeping apartments, and commence living at the rate of about five bales of cotton a week. The ladies come down to dinner the first day, presenting perhaps a slightly seedy appearance. Hoops have not yet been heard of at Kentucky Bend, and the bareges and organdies of last summer's wear look but limp and tawdry, and compare unfavorably with the brilliant silk robes that surround them. Still our family preserves a confident and well-satisfied air; they know "there's a good time coming;" and it is refreshing to observe the defiant glance they cast upon any individual who may chance to look too long or scrutinizingly at their habiliments. The next day the chrysalis has opened, the full-painted butterfly comes forth. "Par" has been to his agents, the ladies have been to Madame Weasel and Mlle. Chargenuff, and silk robes, with fearful flounces, hoops of vast dimensions, point lace, ribbons, and other flummery, are the order of the day.

They breakfast at ten o'clock in the ladies' ordinary, an operation which takes two hours and a half; then they go forth "shopping" (a groan comes in here from every Benedict who reads this paper) until three; then "Adeline the hairdresser," performs the most remarkable feats with their natural locks and the new braids they have purchased, and at half-past four they descend to dinner, arrayed in such magnificence as Solomon in all his glory never began to have the least idea of.

Dinner, which consists principally in an animated contest with the waiters, who won't bring any thing they are sent for, but will persist in carrying every thing off that may chance to be upon the table, lasts an hour or two, and then our ladies adjourn to the parlor, where sitting around in groups, surrounded by their favorite beaux, they gaze affably on the grand crowd of masculine individuals that surround the door, not one of whom knows a lady present, and not one of whom but wishes he knew them all. However, "a cat may look upon a king," and we doubt not that Adam after being kicked out of Paradise, frequently went and peeped longingly into the gate of that garden. So continue to gaze, O Jones, Smith, and Robinson! and envy as you may the happy fellows who have had introductions.

In the evening our ladies go to the French opera, (where the performance is a matter of secondary interest to the struggle of the spectators to out-do each other in richness of attire,) or to theaters, or — it is a fact — to the circus, more tastefully termed the "horse-opera," which last is patronized to a greater extent in this city than any other place of amusement. Then comes supper, oysters and cold turkey, and they retire.

But on Monday evenings the St. Charles is in its glory, for then comes off the weekly "hop." A hop is generally supposed to be a small and informal dancing party, at which the ordinary dinner dress may be worn with respectability.

But as the ladies from Mississippi, and Tennessee, and Louisiana, and Kentucky, and Arkansas, and Milliken's Bend, and every other part of the world, have a large number of party dresses of amazing beauty and richness, and not a very great number of opportunities of displaying them, it so happens that our "hops" at the St. Charles Hotel, are what in other places are denominated full-dress balls. Here you may see the celebrated Mrs. A——, whose first husband left her in possession of such an immense estate, accompanied by her niece, the lovely Miss A——, the belle of Alabama; the dashing and magnificent widow B——, whose four hundred bales a year are her least attraction; the exquisitely beautiful Mrs.

C——, from "the Coast," whose charms of manner and conversation have made her the belle of the St. Charles; Mrs. D——, quiet but observing; pretty Miss E——, from Kentucky; lively Miss F——, the Philadelphia heiress; Mrs. G——, tall, stately, and always tastefully dressed; little Miss H——, with her hair done *à la* Chinoise, and her feet in the same style; the pretty Misses J——, Kentucky beauties; Miss K——, superbly dressed, whose dress-maker's bill is fifteen hundred dollars a year; Madame L——, the "Admirable Crichton" of the female sex, from Mobile; and so on through the alphabet, including all the wealth, fashion, beauty, and extravagance of the South.

It was at one of these gay reünions that dear little Miss B——, one of the prettiest and best girls in the world, asked Butterfield, who stood sweltering in the corner, how he enjoyed himself.

"Hops," replied the sage, "have a soporific tendency, and I do mainly incline to sleep."

"You look," said little Miss B——, "as if a

continuation of these hops would bring you to your bier."

Amos acknowledged the malt by a cheerful guffaw, and looking down on his swelling form murmured, "Larger," and subsided into an arm-chair.

Annually at the St. Charles are given those grand dress balls, which have attained a Union-wide celebrity, and which are well worth travelling over the Union to attend.

Three thousand invitations were issued to the grand ball of this season, and a more crowded, uncomfortable, or magnificent spectacle I never expect to witness. The large suite of rooms were crowded to excess by the most lovely, bewitching, and animated crowd that ever were assembled. Dancing was impossible, they could not do the schottisch, there was not room to pump arms. But it was a glorious spectacle, and so select. I observed among the masses on that gay occasion, the curvilinear proboscis of a well-known Hebrew, who supports himself and contributes to the happiness of mankind by selling shirts on Canal street. He was enjoying himself greatly in a full flow of the finest spirits, when he suddenly "paused in mid career," blenched, and his face assumed a fine expression of humility and confusion.

Looking about for the cause of this appearance, I descried Butterfield gazing upon the victim with a highly virtuous and indignant glance. "What are you looking at the man for?" said I; "you don't know him."

"Don't I?" said Amos in a vindictive whisper; "but I do though. Sell shirts, Sir; sold me a shirt without any ——, well," added he in modest confusion, "when I came to examine it I found it was like Halley's comet, or that fox that Æsop tells about after he got out of the trap."

"You don't tell me that," said I.

"It's so," replied Butterfield; "look here," and pulling me into a corner, he drew from the pocket of his vest a crumpled piece of paper, which thrusting into my hand he whispered, "Read that," and disappeared.

I opened the paper and with some difficulty deciphered the following touching and beautiful

"LINES TO A NISRAELITE."

"Oh! were we but alone, in some region wild and woody,
I'd like to punch your head, old Shylock, Nazareth —— dy.
A cambric shirt to me you once did make a sale of,
But when I took it home, I found you'd cut the —— off;
Whether to make a cravat, or whether to wipe your nose, Sir,
I really do not know, but on me you did impose, Sir.
Like a man without a wife, like a ship without a sail, Sir,
The most useless thing in life, was that shirt without a ——, Sir,
'*Vall it ish vary goot,*' old Shylock Nazareth —— dy,
But I'd like to make you wear it, yes indeed, Sir, would I."

The touching and plaintive character of this *morceau* affected me beyond description; it does, I think, great credit to Butterfield's acknowledged poetical ability.

I should say that there was a great deal of hospitality in New Orleans, which (with some notable exceptions) appears to be graduated pretty closely to the number of bales of cotton annually shipped to that city, by the recipient.* As there

* Thus it has been sagely remarked, that a stranger in New-Orleans must give bale to be well-received, and hence, when a

are a vast number of strangers that do not ship cotton at all, and of course have a great deal of leisure time at their disposal, it follows that "the Rotunda" of the St. Charles is pretty constantly filled. This "Rotunda" forms the centre of the building; it contains about half-an acre of tesselated floor, and is furnished with most comfortable, cushioned arm-chairs. Here, if you take a seat between the hours of eleven A. M. and two P. M., you will have the pleasure of seeing every white male inhabitant of New Orleans, and the majority of those inhabitants of the whole United States that are worth knowing, and with whom you have acquaintance. They come and go, a constant panorama of familiar forms and faces.

The origin of the word "Rotunda" is singular, and not generally known. At the risk of appearing pedantic, I will "norate" it. Many years ago, shortly after the foundation of Rome, a distinguished architect of those days, named Claudi-

resident of the city is observed to be peculiarly kind and attentive to a visitor, they are said "to cotton" to each other.

us Vitellius Smithers, erected the first building that ever was surmounted by a dome. This building was originally intended for a "savings institution," but the Roman that officiated as cashier having left with the funds, it was used successively as a market, dance-house, theatre, and Presbyterian meeting-house, and finally fell into decay and became a mere mass of ruin. Such it remained until the time of the Emperor Alexander Severus, when that monarch one day, accompanied by his courtiers, came down to examine the ruins, with a view to purchasing the lot on which they lay. Here the Emperor's eyes were attracted by the fallen dome, which he gazed on with great curiosity, and finally picking his steps over the stones and rubbish that intervened, he found his way beneath it. The ancient Romans had the same partiality for cheap distinction that animates the modern Yankees; they lost no opportunity of leaving their autograph in all public and private places; the consequence was, that when the Emperor looked up he was amazed at the number of inscriptions that the interior of the old dome presented. It was quite black with ancient and respectable appellations. "Ha!" said the Emperor Alexander Severus, with the air of a man that has made a great discovery, (and with an utter disregard of all grammatical rules,) "*It's been wrote under.*"

His principal courtier, Naso Sneakellius, instantly repeated the remark, with sycophantic reverence to the by-standers, getting about as near it as that stupid official generally did to every thing: "The Emperor," he said "says that this has been a Rotunda. Hats off!"

The Romans all bowed with great solemnity, not having the most dim or distant idea of the joke, and the interior of a dome from that day to this has been called a Rotunda.

I have not told you one-half of the greatness and magnificence of the "St. Charles," but I have not time nor paper to continue. I can only add that it is a most agreeable place to pass the winter, that the proprietor is pleasant and attentive to his numerous families, (when he makes a fortune the St. Charles Hotel will make a great Haul,) and that any one who doubts that it is a delightful place of sojourn had better proceed there at once and have his mind set at rest, which can be done at small expense. Fain would I tell you of "the St. Louis," and of the theatres, and of the opera, and of the "Boston Club," (so called from the sanctity of appearance and dignified demeanor of its members, who are a right nice set of gentlemen, and hospitable to strangers, cotton or no cotton,) but as the man who lost his watch said, "I have no time." The other wonders of New-Orleans for this present, must go unrecorded by this veracious historian, for he is compelled to dessicate.

Adieu, should I write again, you will undoubtedly hear from me.

Respectfully yours,

JOHN PHŒNIX,

Prof., etc.

XVI

MATTERS AND THINGS IN SAN FRANCISCO.

The Limantour (*Le Menteur*) title to about one-half of San Francisco, has lately been confirmed amid weeping, wailing, and gnashing of teeth. John Nugent of the *Herald*, remarked to me that he didn't like the title of my book, "Phenixiana;" said it wasn't a good one. I told him it was as good as any one; *no* title was worth a red cent in this country. (Play on the word *deed*—he! he!) . . . Like unto Mr. Sparrowgrass, I have recently purchased a horse; bought him as "perfectly sound." With the exception of two wind-galls, a splint, and a ringbone, he appears to be. But lo, you! as I was driving him a-down the street this morning, a man

(Johnson, you don't know him) said unto me: "Hello! why don't you get *two* horses for that heavy buggy?—that's too much for one." I know you don't like puns—*I* don't; despise any body that makes them: but I told Johnson I didn't like display, and preferred to drive about in a one-horsetentatious manner. (Play on the word *charger.*) Johnson smiled, and I went off with upright carriage. . . . Since writing the above, a little incident has (actually) transpired that I think will please you. Our little girl, yclept Daisey, fourteen months old, blue eyes, yellow hair, and with a gradually increasing taste for comic almanacs, pleasing to notice, sat upon the floor playing with Harper, Putnam, ye Eclectic, and ye goodlye Knickerbocker, when a sudden ejaculation from the maternal relative, and the spectacle of the baby borne from the room with great precipitancy, attracted my attention. The periodicals suffered. "Never mind," said I to my wife, "I must tell my friend 'Old Knick' of that, and he will rejoice with exceeding great joy to hear it." "I don't see why," said she. "No?" answered I; "why what could be a more satisfactory proof of a literary turn, than to find a child of this precocious age pouring over the columns of the Knickerbocker?" By the way, this reminds me of "suthin" else. Many months ago, when Daisey was but a callow infant, I was afflicted with a grievous cough, and one night, far in the deep watches, I gave vent to such a cough, prolonged, terrific, hideous, that I woke myself, wife, and infant, which last set up a most unearthly and tremendous yell. "There," said my sympathizing partner: "You've gone and woke up the baby." I was wroth at this uncalled-for remark, and replied: "Well, I'm glad of it." There was a moment's silence, and then she asked: "Why?" "Well," said I, "it shows the child has a tender disposition and feeling heart. She is weeping over her father's *coughing*." There was silence at the Mission of Dolores for the space of about half an hour after that. . . . I did not intend to have commenced another sheet, but as I have done so,

I cal'late I had better tell you a small anecdote about Captain Wallen, of the Fourth Foot, which he told me, and I thought at the time, I remember, was worthy of repetition. Wallen started down from the Dalles to Vancouver, to bring up a party of recruits to fight the locomotive Indians. He stopped for the night at the Cascades, in the house of an old man, hight "Uncle Sammy," an inquisitive old fellow, about eighty-six, and deaf as a haddock. After supper the old man, old woman, and Wallen, drew up chairs around a blazing wood fire. The old man immediately commenced applying the brakė, (good expression for *pump?*) "What are ye goin' daöwn to the maöuth of the river for?" "After recruits," replied Wallen, at the top of his voice. "Hey?" "After Recruits!" roared Wallen again. "Can't hear ye." Then the old lady moved round, and putting her mouth to the old man's ear, shouted, in a voice that would have done credit to Stentor after he'd got a little in years: "He's a goin' daöwn — arter re-cruits — sugar — and — coffee — and *sich!*"

. . . One small (Irish) yarn more, and I'll "dry up," *tambien.* Premises: You know a soldier has two dresses — full-uniform and fatigue: the one blazing with worsted embroidery; t'other, dull and sombre-looking. Patrick Hogan, of the Second United States Foot, stationed, in the year of grace, '36, at Tampa Bay, E. F., went forth one day into the wilderness near the barracks, and seating himself beneath a palmetto, essayed to read a small Roman Catholic book called "The Words of Jesus," when "*zoom!*" a yellow-jacket hornet stung him under the left ear. "It hurt," and Pat chased the "*little animil*" for some time, but fruitlessly. Next day, went forth again: same tree; same book; "words," etc.; every thing quiet, when, buzz! buzz! a large brown beetle came flying up. Pat looked at him, and left: "Ah! be J——," said he, "my boy, d'ye think I don't know you in yer *fatagues?*" On reading this over it don't sound as funny as it did when Dr. Byrne of the United States Army told it to *me;* but it's a deuced good story, and if ever we three meet again, I'll have him tell you that, *et al.*, which you never heard before.

XVII.

JOHN RANDOLPH OF ROANOKE.

In an account of the death of John Randolph of Roanoke, which went the rounds of the press a year or two since, it was stated that Mr. Randolph, during his last moments, wrote the word "Remorse" on one of his visiting-cards, and continued to gaze upon it with a melancholy expression until his eyes were closed in death. This statement was dwelt upon with much unction, particularly by the religious papers; the evident effect produced by it being the idea that this great man was troubled in mind, at this solemn period, by the memory of some unrepented and unatoned-for crime. The following passage from "Chittenden's *Western Virginia*" may serve to throw some light on the subject:

"The day after the funeral, a stranger, dressed in deep black, called at the mansion and inquired for Mr. Randolph. He was ignorant of the melancholy event that had occurred, and was profoundly shocked when told of Mr. Randolph's death. He inquired particularly if Mr. Randolph had not asked for him, stated that his business with him had been urgent, and that he had been especially directed to call upon the day on which he arrived, and expressed the deepest regret that he had come too late. On going away, the stranger left his card, on which was engraved, 'R. E. Morse, Culpepper County, Va.' This man was never seen again, and, though frequent inquiries were subsequently made for him, they proved unsuccessful. It was supposed by Burwell that this must have been the agent alluded to by Mr. Randolph in his account of the Cuban affair."

XVIII.

THE GYROSCOPE. A REVIEW.

It is with the greatest pleasure that we acknowledge the receipt from that gifted author, of the "Analysis of Rotary Motion, as applied to the Gyroscope," by Major J. G. Barnard, A. M., Corps of Engineers, U. S. Army. The "Gyroscope" has always been with us a favorite instrument. Of beautifully simple construction, easily managed, and exceedingly gratifying in its results, we know of no machine equally adapted to household use, or more eminently fitted for the amusement or instruction of a small family. It has remained for Professor Barnard, in the interesting treatise alluded to above, to explain, in a simple style, easily comprehended by the merest child, the operation of this instrument, and to show by a clear and beautiful analysis the principle upon which its results depend. There are certain points in "the Analysis," however, on which, with all due humility, we must venture to differ with Professor Barnard; for instance, on page 545 we have the following: "Knowing this fact, we may *assume* that the impressed velocity n is very great, and hence $\cos\theta - \cos a$ exceedingly minute, and on this supposition obtain integral of equations 6 and 7, which will express with all requisite accuracy the true gyroscopic motion." We doubt very much the propriety of making these assumptions; the Mathematics is properly an exact science, and we are by no means prepared to admit the exceeding minuteness of the $\cos\theta - \cos a$, until it is demonstrated to us unmistakably. Again, on page 545, the Professor says: "By developing and neglecting the powers of u superior to the square, we have:

$$\text{“}\sin^2\theta = \sin^2 a - u \sin 2a + u^2 \cos 2a, \text{ etc.”}$$

Allow us to inquire the object of developing the

powers of *u*, provided they are to be subsequently neglected? Can Professor Barnard answer this question? Or, how do we know that *u*, or its powers, *are* superior to the square, which, as every school-boy knows, is next to the sphere, the most perfect of figures? But we have no wish to be hypercritical; our remarks are merely made with the object of discovering the truth, which result deep research only can obtain; as Cicero beautifully remarks, "*De profundis clamavi*," or "out of the deep have I procured a clam;" showing in a figurative manner the necessity that he felt of thorough investigation on the most ordinary occasions. The analysis of Professor Barnard is written in a playful, humorous style, admirably adapted to popular comprehension, and, like the chaste works of Professor Bache, formerly noticed favorably in this journal, contains nothing that could bring a blush on the cheek of the most fastidious, the whole subject being treated in the most delicate manner, and all unpleasant allusions carefully avoided. We cordially recommend to each of our readers to purchase the work for himself and Mrs. Smith, and a copy for each of the children, satisfied that they will be well repaid by its perusal.

XIX.

THE SONG OF "NOTHIN' SHORTER."

BY H. W. TALLBOY.

I transmit to you a heroic poem, the production of the author, Mr. H. Wadding Tallboy, which it strikes me any one might have waited to read, six months at least, and probably longer, with satisfaction and advantage. Several fiiends of mine, who have had a sly peep at the manuscript, declare that "this quaint legend is told with exquisite grace, sweetness, and power!" and I trust you will be of their opinion. You will perceive the moral is excellent, and the general tone unexceptionable; nothing in fact being introduced which could bring a blush upon the cheek of the most fastidious. The main incidents are facts; and thus woven together form a pretty little romance, sweet indeed to dwell upon.

At the Mission of Dolores,
Near the town of San Francisco,
Dwelt an ancient Digger Indian
Who supported his existence
Doing "chores" and running errands,
(When he "got more kicks than coppers.")
He was old and gaunt and ghostly,
And they called him "Step-and-fetch-it."
Old and grim and ghostly was he,
Yet he had a lovely daughter,
Sweet and budding, though not blushing,
For her skin was kinder tawny,
So she really could'nt do it.
But she was a "gushing creature,"
And her springing step so fawn-like
"Knocked the hind sights" off the daughters
Of the usurers consequential,
Who in buggies ride, important,
Rattling past the lonely toll-gate.
Yes, a sweet and fairy creature
Was old "Step-and-fetch-it's" daughter,
And her name was "Tipsydoosen,"
Or ye young grass-hopper eater!

Should you ask me whence this story,
Whence this legend and tradition?
I should answer, "That's my business;
And were I to go and tell you,
You would know as much as I do."
Should you ask who heard this story,
This queer story, wild and wayward?
I should answer, I should tell you,
All the California people,
Pipes of Pipesville, King of William,
Jones and Cohen, Kean Buchanan,
And Miss Heron, sweet as sugar;
And the Chinese, eating birds'-nests,
Well they know old "Step-and-fetch-it."
Near a grocery at the Mission,
Step-and-fetch-it and his daughter
In the sun were once reclining.
Near them lay a whiskey-bottle,
Mighty little was there in it,
For the old man's thirst consuming
Caused that fluid to evaporate.
In his hand old 'Step-and-fetch-it"
Held a big chunk of boiled salmon,
And as fish, bones, all he bolted,
Wagged from side to side his visage,
And with moans, strange, wild, portentous,

Sung the song of "Nothin' Shorter,"
Accompanied by Tipsydoosen,
In four sharps, upon the Jew's-harp.

"Twang a diddle, twang a diddle
Twang a diddle, twang a diddle,
Twang, Twang, Twang, Tum!"

"Nothin' Shorter" was a "digger;"
So am I, and nothin' shorter;
(Thus he sang, old "Step-and-fetch-it,")
And he lived upon the mountains,
Dug his roots and pulled the acorns,
And the rich grass-hoppers roasted.
Happy was he, bold and fearless,
Had no troubles to molest him,
Had no fleas upon his blanket,
For in fact he had'nt got one.
"But one morning gazing earthward,"
He beheld a pond of water
Which he forthwith fell in love with,
And the pond reciprocated.
And they loved each other fondly,
Happy long they were together.

Twang a diddle, twang a diddle,
Twang! Twang! Twang!

Yes, the pond loved "Nothin' Shorter,
Every day she bathed his forehead,
Gave him drink when he was thirsty,
Would have washed him well all over,
Only that would take the dirt off,
And the grease, and yellow ochre,
In which his very soul delighted.
But "they lived and loved together;"
Yes, they lived and loved together
(An original expression)
Till the sun, with fever scorching,
Caused the little pond to "dry up."
Then was "Nothin' Shorter" angry.
Loud he howled, and tore his breech-cloth.
And with fury shrieked and dan*ced*,
As on the sun he poured his curses.
And he cried, "O Scallewagger!"
Which is the Indian name for sun, "Sir,
You have been, and gone, and done it.
It was you dried up my sweet-heart,
Killed the beauteous Muddybottom,
You confess it; you confess it."
And he saw the sun wink at him,
As if to say he felt glad of it.
Then up started "Nothin' Shorter,"
And making quick a pair of mittens
Out of willow-bark and rushes,

With them rent a crag asunder,
Rent a jutting crag asunder,
And, picking up the scattered pieces,
Hurled them at the sun in vengeance,
And so fast the rocks kept flying
That the air was nearly darkened
And obscured, so "Nothin' Shorter"
Could not see but what he hit it.
So he ran and kept on throwing
Stones and dirt, and other missiles,
Till the sun, which kept retreating,
Got alarmed at his persistence,
And behind the western mountains
Hid his recreant head in terror.
But the last rock "Nothin' Shorter"
Threw, fell back on his "*cabeza*,"
And produced a comminuted
Fracture of the cerebellum.

"*Twang a diddle, twang a diddle,*
Twang, Twang, tum."

For some time poor "Nothin' Shorter'
Lay upon the earth quite senseless,
Till a small exploring party
Under Colonel John C. Fremont,
Picked him up and fixed his bruises,

Put on "Dalley's pain-extractor,
And some liquid opodeldoc.
When relieved, though sorely shattered,
He sat up, upon his haunches,
And to Fremont told his story.
Gravely listened that young *savan*,
Wrote it down upon his nóte-book,
Had old Preuss to make a drawing
Representing "Nothin' Shorter"
Throwing boulders; then he gave him
An old blanket and a beef-bone,
And when he asked him for a quarter,
Told him to go unto the Devil.
But far away in eastern cities
Fremont told that tale of wonder;
And a certain famous poet
Heard it all and saw the picture,
Wrote it out and had it printed
In one volume post octavo.
And I wish I had the money
For this song of "Nothin' Shorter."

Twang a diddle, twang a diddle,
Twang! Twang! Twang!

At this juncture, Amos Johnson
Rushed tumultuously from his grocery.

Crying, "Dern your Indian uproar;
Stop that noise and 'dry up' quickly,
Or, by the Eternal Jingo!
I'll ——" here he saw Miss Tipsydoosen,
And the heart of Amos caved in,
As afterward he told Miss Stebbins
That she "just completely knocked him."
Why should I continue longer?
"Gentiles," well ye know the sequel,
How the bright-eyed Tipsydoosen,
Now is Mrs. Amos Johnson;
Wears gipure, and old point laces,
And wont visit Mrs. Hodgkins,
'Cause her husband once made harness.
Yes, a leader of the fashion
Now is "Young Grasshopper-Eater,"
And the ancient "Step-and-fetch-it"
Has a residence at "Johnson's;"
In the back-yard an umbrella
Stuck for his accommodation,
Where he sleeps and dreams fair visions
Of the days of "Nothin' Shorter;"
And the moral of my tale is,
"*To be virtuous and be happy.*"

XX.

THE MASSACHUSETTS DENTAL ASSOCIATION.

Nahant House, Aug. 6, 1857.

While deeply interested in the discussion of the luxurious repast provided for the happy guests of this mansion yesterday afternoon, my attention was diverted by the sound of music of a wild and Saracenic description, resounding from the exterior of the building. The melody appeared to be that portion of the "Battle of Prague" which represents the "cries of the wounded," accompanied by an unlimited amount of exertion on the part of the operator on the bass drum. Hastily rushing to the window, bearing elevated on my fork the large potato from which I had partially removed the cuticle, (Stevens gives us enormous potatoes, it takes twenty minutes to skin one properly,) I beheld a procession, numbering some three or four hundred, all in their Sunday clothes, every man with a cigar in his mouth, slowly and solemnly moving past the hotel. They bore a banner at their head, on which was depicted an enormous cork-screw, or some instrument of that description, with the motto "*A long pull, a strong pull, and a pull all together.*" Judge of my astonishment and delight in recognizing in the beam of this banner, my old friend, the philanthropic tushmaker, of wide-spread dental renown. As the procession reached the front of the hotel, each man threw away his cigar, and having replaced it by a large quid of tobacco, defiled on the esplanade beneath the piazza in a tolerably straight line, and then gazing intently at the windows, opened his mouth, from one auricular orifice to the other, and showed his teeth. Never have I seen so glittering a display. Filled with curiosity, I was about to ask an explanation, when my friend Doolittle from Androscoggin, who had rushed to the window at the same time with myself, saved me from the trouble, by demanding with an incoherent and exceedingly nasal pronunciation, "Why, what on airth is this ere?" "This," replied the courteous Hiram, whose suavity of manner is only equalled by the beauty of his person, "this, sir, is the American Dental Association, composed of members from all parts of both continents, and the British West India Islands." "*Jerewsalem*," said Doolittle, "*three hundred tewth carpenters!*"

It was indeed a thrilling spectacle. To think of the amount of agony that body of men had produced, and were capable of yet producing, to think of the blood they had shed, and of their daring and impetuous charges, after the gory action was over! The immortal charge of the six hundred at Balaclava was not a circumstance to the charges made daily by this three hundred. As Hiram had truly said, these were dentists from all parts of the civilized world and elsewhere. There was the elegant city practitioner, with shiny hat and straw colored gloves, side by side with the gentleman from the country, who hauls a man all over the floor for two hours, for a quarter of a dollar, and gives him the worth of his money. I

Sedan-chairs and Panniers.—*See page 244.*

observed that forty-seven of them wore white hats, and two hundred and sixty-eight used tobacco in some form. There can be no question that this substance is a preservative to the teeth. I observed, in the rear rank, the ingenious gentleman who invented the sudden though painful method of extracting a tooth by climbing a tree, and connecting by a catgut string the offending member with a stout limb, and then jumping down; a highly successful mode of operation, but not calculated to become popular, in the community. He wore buckskin moccasins and did not appear to be enjoying a successful practice.

But while I gazed with deep interest upon the assembly, the band struck up " *Tom Tug*," and away they went. Three times they encircled the hotel, then " with their wings aslant, like the fierce cormorant " swooped down upon the bar, registered their names, and took a grand united Federal drink, (each man paying for himself.) Here toasts and sentiments were the order of the day. " The American Dental Association, like watermen, we pull one way and look another." — "A three dollar cavity, very filling at the price." — "The woodcock, emblem of dentistry — he picks up his living from the holes and passes in a precious long bill." The memory of Dr. Beale, drank standing. These, with other sentiments of a similarly meritorious character were given, and received with great applause.

Having all drank from the flowing bowl, the association again formed in line in front of the piazzas, which were now crowded with a curious and admiring throng, and sang with surprising harmony the following beautiful, plaintive and appropriate chant : —

1.

"Oh, Jonathan Gibbs he broke his tewth
A eatin' puddin', a eatin' puddin'—
Jonathan Gibbs he broke his tewth
A eatin' puddin', a eatin' puddin'.

2.

"Great lumps of suet, they stuck intew it,
Intew it, intew it, intew it, intew it,
Great lumps of suet, they stuck intew it,
As big as my two thumbs."

This chant finished, and the applause subsiding, an air of gravity came over the association, and the president, Dr. Tushmaker, stepping forward, announced that a few pleasing and wonderful performances would now be gone through with, with the object of exhibiting the dexterity acquired by the members of the society. Then turning to the line he gave the command, "*Draw!*" In an instant every one of the association was armed with a brilliant turnscrew. "*Fix!*" shouted Dr. Tushmaker, and each member opened his mouth and attached the fearful instrument to a back tooth. "*Haul!*" screamed the doctor. "Hold, for God's sake," shouted I, but it was too late; three hundred double fanged back teeth, dripping with blood, were held exultant in the air. The association looked cool and collected; there might have been pain, but, like the Spartan boy, they repressed it; the ladies with a wild cry of horror fled from the piazza. "*Replace!*" shouted Dr. Tushmaker, and in an instant every tooth returned to the mouth whence it came, I understood it at once, it was ball practice with blank cartridge — they were all false teeth. Several other interesting exercises were gone through with. A hackman passing by on his carriage was placed under the influence of chloroform, all his teeth extracted without pain, and an entire new and elegant set put in their place, all in forty-two seconds. His appearance was wonderfully improved ; he had been known, for years, as "snaggled toothed Bill," but a new and more complimentary title will have to be devised for him. Wonderful are the improvements of science. At 5 o'clock the procession was reformed, and the band played "*Pull Brothers, Pull*," the association moved off, returning by the Nelly Baker to Boston.

I have never seen three hundred dentists together before, and I don't believe any body else ever did, but I consider it a pleasing and an improving spectacle, and would suggest that the next time they meet they make an excursion which shall combine business with pleasure, and all go down together and remove the snags from the mouth of the Mississippi.

Yours respectably,

J. P ——.

XXI.

THE LEGEND OF JONES.

Nahant House, Aug 10, 1857.

During the past week Nahant has presented an unusually lively and fashionable appearance. On Sunday, nine hundred guests sat down to dinner together at "the House." I wish I could say one thousand, but, like that boy who stated that his father had killed ninety-nine pigeons at a shot, and on being asked why he didn't say a hundred, indignantly replied, "Do you suppose my father would tell a lie for one pigeon?" my habit of exactitude forbids. Our society is composed of people from all parts of the Union; Bostonians, social, affable and particularly kind and attentive to strangers; Western people, cool, *distingué*, and difficult of access; and Southerners, lively, bustling, but close, calculating and abstemious. All enjoy the cool and delightful breezes from the sea, the rides upon the beach, the bathing in the surf, which last is funnier to gaze upon than to actively participate in; the yatching, fishing and other amusements of the hour. Signor Blitz has been here, performing his wonderful feats, and feet more wonderful are nightly displayed in the drawing-room during the progress of our hops. It gives me pleasure to inform you that "the man who parts his hair in the middle," has arrived; he attended the hop last evening and engaged in "the Lancus" with frantic violence, being apparently in great agony from a pair of tight boots. I discovered him in the barber's shop, this morning, lost in a pensive reverie before a looking-glass. He passes much of his time in this way, and won't try sea bathing, or chew tobacco, for fear of injuring his complexion. "The Double Eye Glass Club," (D. I. G. C. they place after their names,) are flourishing; two of them have improved so they can see through their glasses nearly as well as they can without them. It is quite refreshing to see a member take down his glass to read the morning papers, and the haste with which he replaces it if surprised by an outsider. A friend of mine named M——, from New Orleans, who has always had a taste for fashionable life, and in fact has nearly starved himself to death to improve his figure, being anxious to join the club, went to Boston yesterday for the purpose of procuring the tools. Entering a fashionable jewelry establishment he made known his wishes, and a box of double eye glasses was placed at once before him. "What focus would you prefer, sir?" inquired the shopkeeper with immense politeness. "*Window glass*," replied M. solemnly, "I'm not near-sighted, sir, I'm stopping at Nahant." "Oh, exactly," said the jeweler, and he fitted out his customer with great celerity. M. says he is afraid it won't work, the instrument pinches his nose to that extent that he has acquired a nasal pronunciation, and it is painful to him to bid his friends "Good bordig."

Jones has been here! My first interview with Jones was on board the magnificent floating palace which he so ably commands. In other words, Jones is the captain of an old steamboat, and " 'twas there we met, 'twas there we loved, and I confessed " that he could take my hat.

The circumstances were these; I had just got through with an animating altercation with the clerk on the subject of my quarters for the night. Persuaded that my health required sudorific treatment, that individual had bestowed upon me a very small stateroom in close proximity to the boiler where the thermometer would have stood at 212° in the shade. At this I rebelled, and the clerk being obstinate and disobliging, it was only after great exertion, and the intervention of numerous friends, that matters were finally settled on a peaceful basis. While sitting on a sofa in the cabin, reposing on my laurels and hugging the trophy of victory in the shape of a new stateroom key, Jones approached. He is a large gentleman, of perhaps fifty-five years of age, with grizzled hair, prodigious nose, and a most winning expression of countenance, calculated to sour the freshest milk at a single glance. Seating himself by my side, Jones revived the subject of the difficulty, taking, of course, entirely my view of it throughout; then looking at me with a most amiable smile, he said, "You are not a man to get into trouble any how; you have one of them open faces that shows me that your only object in life is to make yourself happy and every one around you happy." My face opened at once; Jones had me; I always flattered myself I had a remarkably ingenuous exprèssion, and was delighted at his ready insight into my character. He then went below to take the clerk to task. Having occasion to light a cigar, I passed by the office and inadvertently overheard the conclusion of his remarks to that individual. "My dear sir," said Jones, "you have one of them open faces that shows me your only object in life is to make yourself happy and every one around you happy!" I saw Jones but once more that evening. He was sitting by the side of a rather pretty, but rapid looking lady in a pink organdie, on a *tête a tête* chair in the after cabin. She appeared to be pleased and interested by the conversation of Capt. Jones. As I passed them on my way to my state-room, I heard him say in soft accents, "You have one of them open faces that shows me your only object in life is to make yourself happy and every one around you happy." I observed that the lady in the pink organdie looked at Capt. Jones on this with a sweet expression, much as if she had a spoonful of Maderia jelly in her mouth, and I retired. Much later in the night I was awakened by the unmistakable sounds of a scuffle of some kind in the vicinity of my state-room. There was much rustling and then a feeble voice said "don't." "Oh," replied a low and soothing tone, "you have one of them open faces that show me your only object in life is to make yourself happy and everybody around you happy." This remark was followed by a noise not unlike the drawing of a cork, but I do not pretend to say that Capt.

Jones kissed the lady in the pink organdie ; I *saw* nothing. The next morning, when we landed from the boat, Jones waited upon that lady on shore. They were about to part, perhaps forever — he gazed tenderly in her face — he grasped her hand — a tear came to his eye, and he was about to speak when I passed them. I am sorry to say that, with unpardonable rudeness, I remarked, "Oh, never mind, Jones, we all know she's got one of them faces," etc., and then swinging my valise violently against his interminable shins, I departed. I think Jones got angry, and have the impression that he cursed and used profanity as I walked away, but I am not positive, and it is a matter of very little importance. Months have elapsed since then and these occurrences had faded from my memory, when happening into the office of this mansion a day or two since, I observed a tall, awkwardly built man, with a prodigious nose, engaged in a discussion with Maine, our jovial bookkeeper. Apparently something was wrong with his bill; he had not been charged enough, perhaps. At any rate, as I arrived the matter was adjusted, and just as I was wondering where I had seen him before, he remarked, "Sir, you have one of them open faces that shows me your only object in life is to make yourself happy and every one about you happy." Fully concurring in this opinion, for Maine is something of an Apollo, I here broke in with —" He has that, Jones." Jones turned, gazed and fled. The Nelly Baker took him to Boston — free, I hope and believe; and I trust I may never see him more. Jones has one of those faces, etc.

The Nahant House is a great institution. I find I have nearly concluded my letter without saying anything about our ladies. They are many and beautiful, like the daisies on the sunny side of Ben Nevis. They don't like their names to appear in print you know, initials are only an aggravation, so I will simply say that the most attractive and beautiful married lady, and the prettiest young lady, are from Boston, the most lively and graceful young lady is from New York, and the most charming widow is from Philadelphia. *Jam satis.*, *etc.*

Au reservoir,

Respectfully yourn,

J. P.

XXII.

REPORT OF A SCIENTIFIC LECTURE.

An intelligent and fashionable audience, consist ing of the members of the Biological Society, their friends, and the representatives of the city press, having assembled, the lecturer was introduced by the Hon. Prurient L. Halfjohn, with a few brief and felicitous remarks; after which, bowing urbanely to the ladies, and directing the summary expulsion of a rude boy who had crawled in at a window without paying, Professor Vaurien commenced as follows:

"In a popular work, which may be found upon the centre-table of every lady, and in the library of every statesman—I need hardly say that I allude to the first volume of Sir Walter Scott's Infantry Tactics—the following striking paragraph occurs:

'The object of the "*about face*" is to face to the rear.'

"The contemplation of the singular fact thus evolved in the simple and forcible language of the great Poet, has developed some considerations upon the constitution of Truth, which I now propose to present perspicuously to your minds. In so doing, the naked truth will be exhibited, with a decent regard for public opinion, and the falsity of the assertion, made in one of the poems of Coleman and Stetson, that 'Truth *lies* in the bottom of a well,' rendered apparent by a course of philosophical reasoning.

"By a beautiful application of the differential theory, the singular fact is demonstrated, that all integrals assume the forms of the atoms of which they are composed, with, however, in every case, the important addition of a *constant*, which, like the tail of a tadpole, may be dropped on certain occasions when it becomes troublesome. Hence, it will evidently follow, that space is round, though, in viewing it from certain positions, the presence of the cumbrous addendum may slightly modify the definity of its rotundity. To ascertain and fix the conditions under which, in the definite consideration of indefinite immensity, the infinitesimal incertitudes, which, homogeneously aggregated, compose the idea of space, admit of the compatible retention of this constant, would form a beautiful and healthy recreation for the inquiring mind: but, pertaining more properly to the metaphysician than to the ethical student, it cannot enter into the present discussion.

"It is here alluded to as the opening to a field of contemplation and investigation worthy the examination of those representatives of the nation, who have, at present, abundant leisure to devote to such vigorous mental exercise. Our immediate business is with the troublesome constant in its generality. We do not need to particularize; as Pliny the Elder remarked of the needle in the hay-mow: 'It will do to reason upon in bulk.' Assuming, for present convenience, that facts are things, let us reason accordingly; deliberately, for time is eternal; and cautiously, for nothing can be more uncertain than facts, and the presence of the peculiar constant adds to the uncertainty instead of annulling it, integrals though facts be. As, in our small but efficient Navy, one man cannot, unassisted, be guilty of mutiny, so cannot his individual volition be creative of fact. In fact, fact cannot be created. It must preëxist, and to that preëxistence, as well as to the fact itself, must be attached and mentally comprehended the variable constant. That mental comprehension must be dull; of the mind that promulges, and of the soul that is impressed by it, both retaining, being integrals, the variable invariable. From these simple considerations we draw the substance of what vain mortals, each with his or her changable constant attached, call Truth.

"Truth involves the inception of its preëxistence, followed by enunciation and comprehension, and accompanied in both mental essences, by homogeneous arrangements of accordant constants of variable constitution.

With this clear view of an hitherto misunderstood conception, its positive applicability to the ordinary affairs of the world is rendered impracticable without an equally lucid consideration of attendant constants too numerous to be readily reconcilable with one another and with the subject under discussion. And under this difficulty has the world existed ever since the beginning of the precession of the equinoxes, and so it will continue to roll on while time shall last, accompanied by its ever-increasing swarm of variable invariables!

"Ingenious apprximations are all that the patient investigator dares to substitute for the remote Truth, which, like the lost Pleiad, every one thinks he can see. So standeth the world gazing agape upon plethoric immensity and saying, 'There is Truth!' The world, here alluded to, is an aggregation of individuals with their respective constants in various states of order and confusion. Suppose a communication from one of these head-quarters of reason and its reception by another: Can condemnation be predicated, or odium exhale from the accidental incompatibility of the attached constants? Hardly. Does approbation confer upon such communication the property of indubitable veracity?" Such were a far-stretched conclusion. Examine well your variable constants, and too often you will detect defects in their co-existent accordance.

"The subject admits of much deep thought and profound study, and is commended to the class before named as an occupation for eternity. These few hints may show the open path to deeper investigation, and those who value TRUTH may pursue it. Meanwhile, let the broad mantle of charity enwrap your own and your fellow-mortals' errors. Seek patiently. Until the end is attained, condemn not rashly. May not your own constant be a little out of order?"

Amid a storm of applause, I was borne by the Hon. Prurient L. into the next room, where the door-keeper was waiting to render his account of the evening. A hasty inspection of his book educed the gratifying fact that the receipts of the night amounted, over and above expenses, to the handsome sum of four dollars thirty-seven-and-a-half cents! But what are net receipts compared with fame!

An embarrassing circumstance has, however, been brought to my notice. The committee of the Bt. who got out the mammoth posters announcing the lecture, in order to secure a full house, rashly pledged in my name, one thousand dollars to the Cabmen's Orphan Society, and the treasurer is even now awaiting the receipt thereof at the door. In this emergency my self-possession does not desert me. I am now busy painting my visage with a burnt cork, and Prurient has turned my coat wrong side out, so that I may pass him under the assumed character of Gumbo Chaff. I shall discontinue lecturing. It has its annoyances. Flint's new hat, which he so liberally lent me, "for this night only," has been used as a spittoon by a reporter during the whole evening. Prurient advises me to leave. He says he will procure me a mission to the Choctaws through his influence with the Sec. of the Int—— (there! I had nearly betrayed his confidence,) with a distinguished person, the S-cr-t-ry of the I-t-r-or, and I will start to-morrow. When you get another letter you will know my whereabouts.

City of Panama, New Granada,
Lion's Den, Oct. 1, 1852.

SQUIBOB.

XXIII.

GREAT RAILROAD PROJECT!

THE BELVIDERE AND BEHRING'S STRAITS UNION RAILROAD.

The foregoing is the title of a road which has become a *fixed fact* in the minds of the projectors.

The proposed road commences at Belvidere, in the State of Illinois, and runs thence in a north-westerly direction to Behring's Straits, *via* Roscoe. It is also proposed to diverge several branches from the main line, the first of which is to be known as "The North Pole Extension Railroad," and by which it is proposed to secure the ice-trade.

The main line crosses the before-mentioned straits by a floating bridge; thence south, by easy grades, and tunneling the Chinese Wall, to Pekin.

At or near Behring's Straits it is proposed to diverge with a branch in a southerly direction to Cape Kamschatka, the said branch to be called the

"Kamschatka Valley Union Railroad." The object of this branch is to secure the seal-trade for the Calcutta market.

It is also proposed to start another branch at or near the same point of divergence, running in a westerly direction to Tobolsk, in Siberia, connecting at that point with an "Underground Exile-escaping Railroad" to the Dead Sea. The said underground road to be built under the immediate supervision of eminent Ohio engineers, they having had much experience in works of that character. The services of Captain Ingraham have been secured as conductor on this road.

From Pekin there will be a branch to Jeddo, crossing the straits near the island of Niphon by an immense Pile Bridge. The object of the branch is to convey troops and munitions of war from the United States to "civilize" and annex the Japanese, and also to secure the Japan-ware trade.

From Pekin will diverge another branch, *via* Cochin China (to secure the fowl-trade), Farther India, Borneo, and Sumatra, to the Gold Mines in

Australia. It is proposed to cross the arms of the sea separating these islands by immense stone culverts of the latest pattern.

The main line then extends to Calcutta, tunneling the Himalaya Mountains, connecting at this point with the "London and Calcutta Union Railroad," and with the plank-road to Booloochistan.

The main line then extends from Calcutta, *via* Bagdad, crossing the Red Sea at *Moses's Ford*, and the great Sahara Desert to Timbuctoo, connecting with the "Niger River Valley Union Railroad" to the coast of Guinea.

The main line then extends through Ethiopia and the Caffre settlements to the Cape of Good Hope, there connecting with the "*Union Balloon Company*," plying between Cape Town and Patagonia.

Thence the main line extends up the west coast of America, *via* Valparaiso and Panama, to San Francisco, with a branch to the Lobos Islands (for the guano trade), and to Astoria, in Oregon. From San Francisco the line extends on a direct course to the place of beginning, with a plank-road to New York city.

It would be useless to descant at any length upon the advantages which this road will possess over all others. A glance at the map will be sufficient to impress upon the mind of the most "general reader" an idea of the stupenduosity of the scheme, and the mines of wealth which will be necessary in order to build it. To the man of business, the extreme facility with which the most distant portions of the globe can be reached should especially commend this project; and to the pleasure-seeker, the ease with which he can be transported to the Maelstrom (which undoubtedly is the greatest watering-place in the world) should make this to appear *the* project of the age; the work which will cause this generation to shine in the very extreme of glory on the farthest limits of time.

We hope soon to announce the successful opening of this great work.

XXIV.

TOPOGRAPHICAL ENGINEERS.

While the bill for reorganizing the Army was under consideration during the last session of Congress, the Military Committee of the House of Representatives addressed a circular to the Chiefs of Bureaus stationed in Washington, requesting their views in relation to the wisdom and propriety of its several provisions. The various letters received by the Committee in reply to their circular were subsequently printed by order of Congress, and a copy of the curious and amusing document thus formed has recently found its way to this country. Its contents are of such an interesting and extraordinary nature, considered in either a literary or military point of view, that it is much to be regretted it was not published in a more accessible form. Stereotyped, and given to the world with a few humorous illustrations, it would have met with an unprecedented sale, leaving Fanny Fern's Leavings, Barnum's Swindle and Wickoff's Love Chase far in the distance.

The *chef-d'œuvre* of this unique document, the richest cream where all is richness, is undoubtedly the letter of Brevet Brigadier-General Joseph E. Totten, Chief of the Corps of Fortification Engineers. As a pompous display of dullness, bigotry and narrow-minded views, it is worthy of the pen of the celebrated Col. Sibthorpe. It would require more time and ability than I have at my disposal to attempt a thorough review of the General's letter. I shall therefore confine myself to a slight fusilade against the most salient point of this redoubtable piece of military engineering.

It will be remembered that the Army Bill above alluded to, contained among other provisions, one "discontinuing the Corps of Topographical Engineers, and transferring its officers to the Corps of Engineers or other corps and regiments." The

Corps of Topographical Engineers, organized in 1838, consists of forty-six officers, most of whom have served in the field, not without some little distinction, and whose scientific skill, not acquired without hard study and experience, has been constantly called in requisition in the construction of military roads, improvement of rivers and harbors, building light houses, establishing boundaries and particularly in increasing the geographical knowledge of the country by explorations of new and comparatively unknown territories. The faithful discharge of these duties requires the utmost familiarity with the higher and more abstruse branches of science, and the young officer engaged in them has the satisfaction of knowing that he is doing something useful for his country, and that his exertions are appreciated by his countrymen. The Corps of Engineers, (commanded by Brevet-Brigadier General Totten,) have no other specific duty in time of peace than to erect permanent for tifications. These works, built of brick, cut stones, dirt and cement, were invented as a system of national defence by an old person named Vauban, some years since, and as he confessed himself (never dreaming of Sebastopol) that the best of them could be captured in forty days, it may be a question, as the boy said when he learned the alphabet, "whether it's worth while to go through so much work to do so little." But, leaving the question aside, it is very evident that the officers of the Corps of Engineers, being constantly employed in this manner, according to a system of unvarying rules, have little opportunity to display any ability beyond that of other stone masons, and the highest stretch of their ambition in time of peace, must probably be to become the happy inventors of some new conglomerate, breccia, putty or other unpleasant stuff spoken of in the works of old Dennis Mahan. I do not allude to the duties of either Corps during a state of war, for the reason that both then, become to some extent, soldiers, lose their distinguishing characteristics and perform nearly identical services. It could scarcely be expected that the Officers of the Topographical Engineers would be contented at undergoing the operation so pleasantly alluded to as "being discontinued," or that they would feel any ecstatic delight at being merged in the Corps of Fortification Engineers, to become manufacturers of permanent fortificacations, dirt pies on a large scale, which, (Sebastopol excepted,) anybody can knock down again in forty days. Such a life holds out little prospect of distinction, and I am persuaded that, no matter how much talent or ability a young man may possess, if, when he has completed his education, you give him a fixed salary for life, and make him a stone mason, a stone mason he will remain, and never be heard of in any other capacity. But Brevet Brigadier General Totten does not view the matter at all in this light. Believing that his corps is the embodiment of every thing that is useful and improving; that the manufacture of putty is the most scientific employment under the sun; or in the words of another old lady, "there is but one what-d'ye-call-it, and he is its thingumbob,"— he utterly objects to the introduction of the unfortunate topographers, on the ground that their capacity is not sufficient to master the tremendous duties of the Corps of Engineers, and that it would be doing his officers great injustice to associate with them men of such inferior ability. And how do you imagine he proceeds to prove the topographical inferiority? By quoting the graduating standing of these officers at the Military Academy at West Point.

Says the General — "Those cadets only who graduate at, or near the head of a class at West Point, are promoted as Lieutenants in the Corps of Engineers; the succeeding cadets are promoted in the Topographical Engineers and Ordnance." And then to render clear the injustice of merging the two corps, he produces statistics to show that the average graduating standing of the Officers of Engineers is represented by the number $2\frac{1}{2}$, while that of the inferior Topographers actually amounts to $11\frac{1}{4}$. (One of the officers having unhappily stood 55th, was promoted in the Infantry, and transferred.) This is indeed a fearful distinction. Since the publication of this alarming discovery, a friend of mine who has the misfortune to be a Topographcial Engineer, (but who constantly wears a citizen's dress, for fear some one will find it out,) tells me he never walks the street without fancying a huge $11\frac{1}{4}$ chalked between his shoulders, attracting the public attention and obloquy. If he meets an Officer of Engineers, he reverently makes way, respectfully murmuring $2\frac{1}{2}$; and he has entirely lost the power of looking out for No. 1, so absorbed is he in the thought of No. $11\frac{1}{4}$. It may be considered a very fair method of classification to take an officer's graduating standing at the Military Academy as a guage of his mental calibre for the remainder of his existence, possibly the rule might work to admiration in a corps where no incentives were held out for study or improvement: but to show that in the army at large it has, like "Taylor's Theorem," its failing cases, allow me to adduce one or two instances.

The present Secretary of War, Hon. Jefferson

Davis, who, I presume, General Totten would not consider quite destitute of ability, graduated twenty-third in his class, and the present Minister to China, Hon. Robert M. McLane, late M. C. from Maryland, formerly of the Topographical Engineers, and by no means an idiot, graduated thirty-seventh in the class of 1837. But the Corps of Topographical Engineers was only formed in 1838, while the Engineers date from the time when Noah, sick of the sea, landed and threw up a field-work on Mount Ararat. I remember well a time-honored legend at West Point, which told how one of the earlier classes at that institution was composed of but *two* members. At their final examination, one was sent to the Board to demonstrate the 47th problem of Euclid; but after a little hesitation he confessed his inability to draw the figure, though he felt confident he could make the demonstration. The second here rose, and diffidently remarked, that though he could not demonstrate the proposition, he was able to draw the figure. This division of labor was accordingly made, the figure drawn in a style of unrivaled elegance by the one, who was placed head in drawing, and forcibly demonstrated by the other, who was placed head in mathematics.

Both gentlemen were deservedly promoted in the Corps of Engineers. If this story be true, and I certainly do not vouch for it, the singularly small number representing the graduating standing of the Corps of Engineers may be accounted for.

But if West Point standing is referred to as a means of judging of the ability of an experienced officer, why not go farther back in his antecedents? Why not, on Brevet Brigadier General Totten, prove that the officers of the Corps of Engineers at their first introduction to this world of sin and sorrow, weighed from 12 to 16 pounds each, while the Topographical babies were but puling weakly things, averaging at the best but seven and a quarter? Why not refer to the Sunday Schools, where the little Engineer Infants at the early age of five, could repeat with fluency the Apostles' Creed, the Lord's Prayer, and the Ten Commandments, while the poor little Topogs (weighing then scarcely eleven and a quarter) could scarcely get through their A B — A B'S, and ask for sugar? It strikes me illustratious chief of a Super-topographical Corps, that these researches would be eqnally apposite and convincing.

The letter of the Brevet Brigadier General, contains many other funny statements, besides the statistics: the document contains many funny letters besides the Brevet Brigadier's, but I have no time to allude farther to them at present. I would merely suggest to a discerning pnblic, the propriety of having the whole published by subscription, elegantly bound in gilt and morocco, after the manner of the Knickerbocker Gallery. Then with the proceeds, by the side of that limpid lake, from whence the calm waters of Salt River placidly meander to the sea, I would have erected a beautiful cottage, in form, a mural castle, with the number 2½ in brazen block letters above the portal. Here in quiet contemplation over what he has done, and in the tranquil enjoyment of his self esteem, Brevet Brigadier General Totten might pass the remainder of his days in happiness and peace. But he should not be allowed to write any more letters!

Respectfully, your obedient serv't,

CONRAD POMPON,

Capt. Light Brigade, 11¼ Division,

California Militia.

XXV.

ON CLIPPER SHIPS.

I send this by special current express, calculating that it will drift along a few days ahead of us; and you can have it all ready to put in, while we are within the usual "two hours" sail of the port for twenty-four days. Don't forget also to mention the fog, loss of sails, heavy weather, etc., and particularly "the light and baffling head-winds for a couple of months." But you can regulate that by the length of our voyage. No matter if you do make a little error of ten or fifteen days in our favor, in reporting us. If not noticed, we won't correct it; but if it is, then pitch into the compositors, and call it a typographical error.

* * * * * * * *

She is one hundred and fifty tons register, and carries two thousand, as measured in Boston, with the measurer's thumb inside the callipers, which (the thumb) being much swollen and tied up in a rag, may have made a few feet difference in the measurements; but that don't amount to much. Her extreme length on deck is five hundred and ninety-seven and a half feet; eight feet breadth of beam; two hundred feet deep; twenty-four feet between decks. Her bow is a great rake, and the head is composed of a female carved figure, with one thumb resting on the extreme tip of her nose, fingers extended in the act of gyrating; the first finger of the left hand in the act of drawing down the lower lid of the eye; which the captain explains to us as a simile from the Heathen Mythology, denoting curiosity on the part of the figure, to ascertain if any body discovers any thing verdant.

The "*Highfalutin*" is finished with the patent "*Snogrosticars*," indicating the millenium when it comes. She is rigged after the recent invention of Captain Blowhard, which consists of three topsail-yards on the bowsprit, the halyards leading down through a groove in the keel, up through the stern windows, and belay to the captain's to-bacco-box. She has also the "*skyfungarorum,*" a sail something like a kite, which is set in light weather about seventy-five feet above the main-truck, and made fast by a running double hitch under the binnacle and aft through the galley, and belayed to the cook's tea-pot. It is sometimes (when the captain carries his family) made fast to the baby-jumper. Her windlass is rose-wood, in-laid with clam shells. She has also a French roll capstan with musical bars. The caboose is elab-orately carved with gilt edges, a Pike county gal-ley-sliding telescopic stove-pipe, of gutta-percha, and a machine for making molasses candy for the sailors.

XXVI.

A LETTER OF CREDIT

Aug. 24, 1856.

My Only Benson: — Your suggestion about the revolting pistols, is highly approved by me, and I wish to improve a little on it, by purchasing also, a clarionet (E. flat) for Marlin, and a piccolo, or octavo flute for yourself. With these dulcet instruments, you and he can sit on the bridge, during the mid-watches of the autumnal nights, and breath forth your saddened spirits in a flood of melody, which shall charm the marine inhabitants of Walewski creek, and make the angry and perturbed nature of the murderer Bell, as soft as mercurial ointment. Please send the money for the pistols and musical instruments, and they shall be forwarded without delay.

For the	Colt's Revolting pistols, for Marlin,	$60
"	" " " Benson,	30
"	1 E. flat Clarionet, ...	10
"	1 Piccolo, ...	10
"	Extra reeds, ...	1
"	Music, a few concerted pieces in B. Minor, arranged for clarionet and piccolo,	10
	Total	$121

I have not the money by me, or I would advance it as you request.

You could not have supposed the United States Government would furnish arms for the use of overseers on a military road. Do they furnish them for the officers of their armies? No, by my faith, those warriors pay for their own swords; they purchase their own habergeons and surcoats, their targets and bucklers, and if they are fain to indulge in the luxury of a Colt's revolter to strap upon their posteriors, (there to hang in inglorious idleness, for aye,) they have to borrow the money from their friends for that purpose.

Fain would I furnish you and the gallant Marlin each with a suit of Milan armour of tempered steel, inlaid with arabesque work of fine gold; Helmets of the same, with a crest of marabout feathers containing four at $1.25 each, swords, shields (with a device representing Bell fishing off Walewski Bridge) habergeons, battle-axes, daggers of mercy; and surcoats and lutes with broad blue ribbon at 3*s*. per yard for your ladies' bower, but I have'nt got the money to spare, and well I am not, if ye seek to come forth in martial guise, your coffers are far better able to supply your armament than is my poor pantaloons pocket. I counsel you therefore, to purchase what you may wish, or make unto yourselves bows and arrows withal to defend yourselves after the manner of our ancient forbears. As to Bell, have I not written unto the sheriffs of Stillacoom and Olympia, praying that he may be suddenly and quickly removed from our midst.

The rope will be sent, the gimbolet is enclosed, (on the outside.) Make more than 2600 feet per week; and believe me to remain,

With deep admiration,

Your affectionate friend,

G. H. D.

XXV

PANNIERS.

Portland, Sept., 20, 1856.

SAY OLD FELLOW: — You've got a way lately of laying back there at Astoria, and imagining all sorts of things which you think would save you the slightest trouble or inconvenience, and sending off orders for them with all the imperiousness of Aldiborontsphoscophornis, when ordering Rigdum-Funnidos to chop off the head of Chrononhotonthologos. What in thunder do you mean? I send the things this time, but request you to get rid of the habit; it grows on you, like an appetite for liquor. All but the pannier's, ha, ha! In the venerated name of Sancho Panza, where did you read about pannier's? The word is suggestive of Dapple Cork trees, Andalusian maids, bandits and sech. Why, ignorant dweller at the corners of Clay and Montgomery, (up stairs) do you know that for eight years I have done little or nothing but travel through California and Oregon with pack trains, during which time I have seen over 4000 mules packed, with over 800,000 pounds of merchandise, while upwards of 4,000,000 oaths and profane execrations were vented at them, and yet never in my life saw a — ha ! ha ! *a pannier.* And do you suppose that I, an old and experienced packer, to whom a hair sinch is as familiar as a tooth-brush, will permit you, having but three mules to pack, to use — a — ha ! ha ! (excuse me) a,— ho ! ho ! (really I can't help it) a — — panniers ! a primeval implement probably used by Balaam to save himself a little trouble in packing his jackass. No, sir. Take a lash rope, double it equally, lay it over the saddle, put an equal weight on each side, and turn up the ends, then take your sinch, and draw it tight over the pack in various directions and fasten the ends to the horns of the saddle. Panniers, indeed,— would'nt you like a sedan chair? Panniers, young man, are only raised in Chili and Peru and other Catholic countries, by the peons and chulos, etc., to carry fruit to market. I have seen them myself in Valpariaso, teeming with the luscious grape, the fragrant strawberry, and the rich and juicy buckwheat cake. But *you* can't have any Panniers. No, sir. You are, however, permitted to look at them — te he! (*See page* 200.)

Your oats were sent by the last boat. The Multnomat resumes her trips to-morrow. We are all disgusted by the non-arrival of the mail steamer Columbia, expected here last night — oh! yes! Have I "thought to make an extract from the letter of the Secretary of War?" No. I haven't thought to make any such extract. You had plenty of opportunity to make an extract if you wanted to, when you were here; if you want any extract now, you can get Lubin to make it. It is not at all in my line! Have I a copy of the act making the appropriation and of the advertisement inviting proposals? Yes, I have a copy of the act, and of the advertisement, and I mean to keep 'em.

Have you got them? If you haven't *don't* you wish you may get 'em?

Good-bye, he — ha! Panniers!

Yours, truly,

SQUIBOB.

CPSIA information can be obtained
at www.ICGtesting.com
Printed in the USA
LVHW040022180422
716440LV00005B/507

9 783752 590524